Pirates in Paradise

Published by Sanibel Press www.SanibelPress.com
318 E Orange Street, Altamonte Springs, Fl 32701

Second e-published by Sanibel Press
Second print publishing March 2006
Random 2004, 2005, 2006

Cover art by Sanibel Press
Cover illustration Copyright © by Sanibel Press 2006

LINN
RANDOM

PIRATES IN
PARADISE

2006

Pirates in Paradise

Praise for Pirates in Paradise by Best-Selling Author
Linn Random

FIVE ANGELS—FALLEN ANGEL REVIEWS

"Want a book you can not put down until you read every last page? *Pirates in Paradise* by Linn Random is just that book. I said I would read a few pages and quit for the evening; what a joke! I never stopped reading until it was over. This is a Recommended Read, and you've GOT to get this one. It's definitely a keeper." *Fallen Angel Reviews of Pirates in Paradise*

FIVE ANGELS—SECOND FALLEN ANGEL REVIEW

"Pirates in Paradise delivers an action-packed plot, which is sure to please fans of romantic suspense. In just over 100 pages, Ms. Random has managed to fashion enjoyable characters with surprising depth and a fast moving storyline. This is a quick read that manages to engage readers immediately. The conclusion lives up to the excitement of the rest of the story and will have readers smiling at the end."

Fallen Angel Reviews of Pirates in Paradise

FIVE BLUE RIBBONS—ROMANCE JUNKIES

"Pirates in Paradise by Linn Random is full of action and suspense. Hot and steamy! The reader will not be disappointed by this author. As a reviewer, I wouldn't mind seeing another book of this magnitude."

Romance Junkies Review of Pirates in Paradise

PIRATES IN PARADISE

The Bronco made a hairpin turn coming to a full stop directly in front of them.

Haley glimpsed a silhouette of a broad shouldered man dominating the driver's side of the vehicle. The driver sat motionless. Time stopped. A frightening premonition swept over Haley, warning her with a fresh new fear, she couldn't name.

The door opened. A tall man stepped out and headed toward them in a catlike stride. Dressed in a black T-shirt and black jeans, his skin glistened bronze in the moonlight. Haley caught her breath at the sight of his broad shoulders. He was menacing and she knew to be afraid. Watching his approach, Haley said under her breath. "This is your friend?"

"That's him," Frank answered with a hard gasp of air.

Stepping under a streetlight, the stranger's short, dark cropped hair glistened in the yellow-white light. A light breeze ruffled one lock forward and he swept it back with a large hand.

Haley noted his classically handsome face, his aquiline nose and square jaw. Darkness obscured the color of his eyes. Small drops of moisture clung to his damp forehead and she saw an inherent strength that seemed vaguely familiar.

Hardly giving Haley a glance, he jumped without being asked into the boat. With the craggy look of an unfinished sculpture, he bent his head down to take a better look at Frank's arm. "You didn't tell me you were shot."

"Yeah, well, you can drop me off at the hospital then and get out of town. By the way, this is Jenna Rollins. Jenna, this is Jack Morgan."

With the moonlight against Jack's profile, he stood well over six foot, and possessed a sensuality that was almost frightening. He nodded at her. His generous lips parted to give her a dazzling display of straight white teeth.

Haley stood stupidly still, knowing she was the source of this night's evils. She looked down. Men had died because of Jenna's lies and her silence. They would never understand she had been trapped into assuming her twin sister's identity; now, there was no way out.

ALSO BY LINN RANDOM

Lights, Camera. Murder!
Your Cheatin Hearts
Pirates in Paradise

Watch for these future best sellers from Linn Random in
2006
Black Waters
Haunted Hearts
Cold River Murders
Mourning Song

To my sister-self, Shelley Wright, who has been a friend and an inspiration. Shelly is a friend who has kept me grounded when I needed to feel safe and allowed me to soar when my heart called me to adventure. My wish for everyone is to have a friend like Shelley. I am blessed to have her in my life.

PROLOGUE

Clutching the address in her hand, Haley looked out her windshield at the neon sign and wondered if she had the right address. Swallowing hard, she re-read the neon sign, 'The Stardust Motel.' The 'r' and 'o' bulbs were dark and made twisted words of the signage. She shuddered. What was her twin sister, with her glamour party girl lifestyle, doing in a run down seedy side of Miami's underbelly?

Two women in wigs, heavy makeup and mini-skirts stood under the motel sign. In the darkness, she watched one flick a cigarette onto the street and gave a casual glance in her direction.

Haley took a shallow breath and turned off the engine of her small compact car. The loss of the familiar engine's purr emphasized her isolation from safety and protection. Her fingers wrapped tight about her car keys, she slipped her shoulder strap purse over her right shoulder and she stepped out of the car. She crossed to the door of Room 23 and knocked.

"Jenna?" she said in a hushed tone as she rapped a second time. Small chips of paint fell to her feet. "Jenna, it's me, Haley. Open the door."

Concern gave way to frightful irritation. Had she driven from Vero Beach to Miami on another one of Jenna's classic wild goose chases?

She knocked at the door a third time. Just as she was about to turn to leave, the door opened.

"Oh my God," Haley cried.

Jenna held onto the door, as if she needed it to stand. Her blue eyes were wide with terror, tears tracking down her cheeks, her skin was ashen. Jenna's expensive clothes always so carefully kept were rumpled about her small frame as though she'd slept in them for days.

Jenna reached out and pulled Haley into the room, her grasp surprisingly strong. She closed the door, taking time to slide the safety lock chain back into place.

"Jenna, what's wrong?" Haley touched Jenna's shoulder.

Jenna wiped her tear-stained face. "I can't tell you, "she whimpered. Her delicate shoulders shook with each small sob. "But I need you to help me."

"How?" Haley asked simply, pulling her sister into her arms. Whatever frightened Jenna, Haley knew she would help; this, after all, was her sister. With a choking cry, Jenna tore herself away from Haley and curled onto the bed. It creaked and sagged from age and years of abuse.

Tears glistened on Jenna's perfect, heart shaped face. "Haley, I'm in so much trouble."

"Is it Ricky?" Haley asked between sobs. She had met Jenna's boyfriend only once.

"Yes. No." Jenna's voice cracked. She sat up and wiped her face before looking at Haley, her expression desperate. "Look, I need you to be me for a couple of days. Just until I can get a few things straightened out."

Haley stared at her sister. "You can't be serious! We aren't kids anymore. We can't just trade places. What's going on? Honey, whatever it is, I'm sure we can figure something out."

"It's best you don't know." Jenna sobbed. Tears blinded her eyes and chocked her voice. "Look, I've made arrangements.

You'll be perfectly safe. Haley, please, I really need you to be me for just a few days."

"Jenna," Haley said losing patience, "Come back with me to Vero. We'll figure something out."

"No!" Jenna cried, "And you can't go back there either, not now! Please, please, it's a matter of life and death. You have to help me! For both our sakes!"

A rap knock at the door startled both of them. Haley jumped. An icy fear twisted around her heart.

"Here take my cell phone. Keep it," Jenna whispered, pressing the phone into Haley's small palm. She backed away from Haley. "I have to go to the bathroom. I'll be right out. Answer the door. It will be okay."

"Hurry," Haley urged her sister as she accepted the cell phone. Without giving it a second thought, she slipped it into her skirt pocket. "Whatever this is, we'll figure something out."

Jenna nodded and hurried to the bathroom. Haley went to the door and opened it.

Two men in dark suits stood outside the door, the dark look in their eyes as dark as their black suits. Behind them was a SWAT Officer pointing his assault rifle at her head.

"You will be safe now, Miss Rollins," the oldest man, about forty, said as he pushed past her. His partner, a tall black man, followed.

"Who are you?" Haley demanded.

"I'm Frank Porter of the U.S. Marshal's office. This is my partner Jim Brody." With thinning brown hair and hazel eyes, he cleared his throat and said, "I want you to know you're doing the right thing. We're here to protect you."

"You don't understand," Haley protested as three more

members of the SWAT Team pushed into the room. "I'm not...."

A SWAT Officer brushed past her toward the bathroom. In black BDU combat fatigues with bullet proof vest, a gun shoulder high, he used his heavy boots to kick the bathroom door open. He pointed his gun to where Jenna should have been standing.

"All clear," he shouted and dropped his rifle to his side.

The two federal agents nodded and placed their guns in their holsters.

Haley swallowed hard, fear knotting inside her. All clear? Where was Jenna? She stepped forward to look inside the bathroom. Empty. Jenna was gone. Only the frosted half open window told of her passing. Where had she gone? Why? Jenna had escaped, leaving her with two US Marshals.

"I don't understand," Haley stammered turning back to the men. "Why are you here?"

Porter's brow darkened and he stared unsympathetically. "You know why we are here, Miss Rollins, we've come too far to play anymore games. Now, gather your things. You're coming with us."

Haley grabbed her purse; there was nothing more in the room that belonged to either twin. When Frank Porter reached for her elbow to lead her out, she pulled away. Passing her car, she pointed to it. "My car. You can't just leave it here."

"Jeff," Frank Porter called out to the head of the SWAT Team. "Have that vehicle impounded."

Without waiting for the police officer to answer, he shoved Haley into the back seat of a sleek sedan.

Two minutes later, they were racing out of the parking lot and away from the motel. She sat silent as the sedan raced through the dark streets of Miami.

In her life, she had never even received a parking ticket. Now she was surrounded by U.S. Marshals careening into the night.

Where had Jenna gone? Why had she run? Fearful images piled up in Haley's mind as she remembered her sister's last desperate whisper, "Be me!"

CHAPTER ONE

Haley laid in the middle of the king size bed confused and angry in a plush upscale Fort Lauderdale neighborhood. At least, that's where she thought she was. She wasn't sure. She wasn't sure of anything. She hadn't stopped shaking since the Marshals had burst into Jenna's room. No one seemed to notice and if they had, they didn't seem to care.

Throughout the last several hours, Haley's moods had swung between being furious at her sister's sinister involvement in something so serious it had brought in the FBI and U.S. Marshals Service to a sense of helplessness and stark terror for her sister's safety, giving little thought to her own. The hurried drive through the dark streets of Miami remained a blur.

Upon arriving at their destination, the Marshals informed her, she was at a safe house. She felt anything but safe.

The two story elegant mansion was palatial and the Federal Marshals had wasted no time in rushing her inside.

Frank Porter took her to the second floor. Perhaps to fill in the empty space between them, he had informed her while climbing the grand marble stairwell that the home had been seized through tax evasion. It was now used for high ranking federal officials and on occasion as a 'safe house' by the Federal Government.

After directing her to an elegant bedroom, Frank had offered her a wardrobe of silky nightgowns. She had muttered thanks but rejected the lot of them opting instead to lie uncomfortably in her own clothes. Did they even imagine she would be able to sleep? She stared at the ceiling trying to understand why Jenna had left her to the Federal Agents?

Reaching into her right pocket, she clutched her sister's Kodiak cell phone. It was her lifeline to Jenna. The first moment she was alone, she had checked the cell and was relieved to find it had a full charge though Jenna had wiped the menu clean of contacts, history and the address book. She could do nothing but wait for Jenna's call.

A warm tropical breeze gushed into the room, carrying with it a heady tropical scent of Hibiscus and exotic flowers. Unable to sleep or lie in bed another minute, she rose from the bed. The marble floor felt cool and smooth.

Restless and with nothing to do but worry, she slowly crossed the room and stepped out onto the balcony. The balcony was spacious and stretched across the back of the house. No other lights brightened the darkness and she had the distinct feeling she was alone on the second floor.

Close to her, the lush and carefully kept grounds were landscaped with majestic royal palms and stunning tropical plants and foliage. Thanks to taxpayer dollars no doubt, she thought grimly. Several hundred yards away, she noticed a boathouse but its interior was obscured in dark shadows.

From where she was standing, she could clearly see the intercoastal waterway. The intercoastal stretched from the Carolinas to Miami. Shards of moonlight danced atop the slow moving waters. In the distance, dark silhouettes of small boats listed and swayed in the current.

The tropical vista did little to soothe her frayed emotions. Her sister's frantic plea echoed in her mind, and too many unanswered questions vied for her attention. She could trust no one.

Feeling older than her 26 years, Haley looked across the exquisite expanse of lawn for answers. About to return to the bed, she caught a shadowy figure scurry from one small tree to another. She slapped her hand over her mouth to hold the scream inside.

"It's only the shadows," she said in a whisper, too frightened to say the words aloud. "I'm safe. No one is out there."

Icy fingers crawled up her spine. Instinctively, she stepped back into the shadows of the balcony and waited, not sure what she was waiting for. Long breathless minutes passed. Gradually, the tranquility once again descended upon the estate. She couldn't shake the sense that something was terribly wrong.

It was late, she reminded herself. I'm tired and with the moon so bright, it's too easy to imagine shapes in the darkness. It's my imagination she told herself silently. Then, she saw it again.

Dark figures emerged from the bushes and darted across an open space to the shadows of three stately Royal Palms. The image was unmistakable. It was a man. He was carrying something slender and long under his arm. He carried a gun.

Unable to move her legs, she stood frozen as the figure motioned into the darkness. Terror rose like bile to her throat, as she watched three more figures emerge from the darkness. They ran toward the house.

Finding her legs beneath her, she ran through the bedroom, grabbed her purse off the dresser and as fast as she could ran down the long corridor. "Help!" she cried at the top of the stairwell, "Hurry!"

Instantly Porter, Brody and two more agents rushed into the foyer and looked up at her. "Men are coming toward the house!" She cried, "I saw them from the window. They have guns!"

All four men pulled out their revolvers. Like a precision drill team, they turned, positioning their backs to one another. The quatrain covered each entryway into the foyer. Brody aimed his gun toward the front door; the two FBI Agents each pointed their weapons into either room off the foyer. Closest to her, Porter aimed his gun toward the back of the hallway.

"Quickly, Jenna," he urged her as he reached for the ornate hall phone. He held it to his ear and immediately returned it to its cradle. "Phone lines are down," he said evenly. His face was grim.

Brody pulled out his cell phone and hit several buttons. "The house is under attack. We need backup. NOW!"

Halfway down the marbled staircase, Haley felt her legs giving way. Frightened, she clutched the banister and began an agonizing descent. The cold look in the men's eyes told her the situation was desperate. They were armed and prepared to protect her.

Haley looked to Frank. He came toward her; his hazel eyes were dark but confident. He tried to smile but the grave expression eclipsed any false guarantee of safety.

"Don't worry, Jenna," his voice cool and measured, "we'll keep you safe."

Haley heard the sound of glass break in a room to her left. She screams as a barrage of bullets spayed through the room. Porcelain vases, lamps, and furniture shattered and fell broke in its rain of fire. The two Marshals fired directly at the intruder. Then one of the agents fell, and his gun slid across the foyer to the stairwell.

Frank Porter pulled him behind the wall. He looked up to Haley on the stairwell and motioned for her to crouch against the banister.

"Get her out of here!" Brody shouted at Frank, as he fired shots into the room.

Mesmerized by the scene and too frightened to move, Haley looked through the railing, her fingers frozen, wrapped around the bars she was holding.

She saw the hesitation in Frank's eyes but he nodded. "Come on," he yelled, pulling her down the stairs. With a hard shove, he pushed her down the back hallway.

"Run!" he screamed shoving her through the kitchen door. Fleeing the sound of gun fire, Haley ran through the ultra modern kitchen. Frank shadowed her as she raced toward the back door.

"The others!" Haley cried with a backward glance to the foyer. The sound of rapid fire caused her to flinch with each explosive discharge.

"Move," Frank shouted without apology, "My job is to keep you safe!"

Passing by her as they rounded the island stove, and Frank grabbed her wrist and pulled her out the kitchen door. Once outside he stopped. He brought the barrel of his gun shoulder high and looked first left then right before dragging her across the lawn.

Haley stumbled trying to keep up with him. Her only hope rested in the man running in front of her; guiding her through the darkness toward the intercoastal waterway and away from the house.

Small bushes and sharp palmettos tore at Haley's dress as she ran after him down a narrow hedged stone walkway away from the gun fire. All through the upscale community came the frantic alert of neighborhood dogs. Abruptly, the gunfire stopped. The silence was deafening, more frightening than the rapid discharge of furious combat.

Frank turned toward the house. His expression was grim. The gun battle was over. His friends, his comrades lay dead or dying and she felt responsible. She bit her lip; her stomach twisted in sickening wave after wave of terror.

"Quiet," he cautioned her in low tones. The soft warning carried with it the reality of imminent danger. "They don't know we have left the house. They're probably are searching for you now."

Soft tears streamed down her face and her hands were shaking. Her body was cold with terror.

"We're almost there," Frank told her with a voice filled with strength and cool assurance, "all I need you to do is move as quietly as you can."

Haley nodded and blindly followed him down the narrow path leading to the boathouse. Reaching the protective screen enclosure, Frank slowly opened the door and scanned the interior. Nodding, he motioned her inside. He moved quickly through the dark interior and slammed the palm of his hand on a hydraulic lift. Immediately, stainless steel cables moaned and twisted as they lowered a 33 foot Wave Dancer speed boat into the water. As quickly as the steel rods sang, they stopped. The sleek racer was safely lowered into the water.

The powerful engines of the Wave Dancer were poised, her long lines glittering metallic red and dark blue in the moonlight. Frank jumped into the center of the sleek Cigarette, and held out his hand for her to join him. Haley leaped from the dock into Frank's arms. He firmly sat her on a side seat and began flipping switches. The Wave Dancer roared to life.

Over the engine's roar, Haley heard the excited sound of voices rushing toward the boat house. She grabbed the back of her seat as Frank jammed the throttle down. The high-speed cigarette jettisoned backward into the water way. With a lightning burst of speed the Wave Dancer exploded from the channel as Frank steered the boat away from the mansion.

The powerful engines sent a spray on either side of her bow and sent a rough wake to either side bank. They passed the back of the safe house and she heard gunfire over the power boat's engines. The sheer acceleration caused the Wave Dancer to jump high over the water in a rapid series of bouncing jerks.

Haley clung to the seat. Her heart pounded. Her eyes transfixed with horror as a small bridge appeared. She didn't need to have Frank tell her to duck as the Wave Dancer slid easily through the tight passage and shot like a missile to the other side.

Frank gave her a quick glance. "You okay?"

Haley nodded. It was all she could do to keep herself steady at the boat's breakneck speed. Frank's turned away from her, focusing his full attention on maintaining the cigarette's course in the center of the channel.

Residential homes and multimillion dollar winter palaces of the rich and famous changed to dock-front restaurants, marinas and towering hotels. Pink, blue and bright yellow lights became multicolored streamers against a black sky. Onboard, desperate minutes passed as quickly as the hotels and marinas. At last, the Wave Dancer broke free of the intercoastal; Frank took a hard left, sending the boat into the open Atlantic. The cigarette sustained its reckless speed until the lights of Miami glittered far in the distance.

Suddenly, Frank eased off the throttle and brought the Wave Dancer to a smooth stop. Ocean waves lapped the fiberglass hull and the 9,000 pound cigarette bounced on the sea like a piece of drift wood. Fighting nausea, Haley looked to the glittering Miami skyline. For the moment, they were safe.

Frank fell back against the seat and gave her a sad smile. Haley had no idea the high price her safety had cost him. He had saved her life.

"Thank you," she said softly and gently touched his arm. The light in his eyes acknowledged her gratitude.

It wasn't until that moment did Haley notice the bright red stream of blood cascading down his forearm. In his attempt to get her to safety, he had been shot!

"You've been injured," she cried. She crossed the space between them and gently touched his arm to get a better look at his wound. The blood looked black in the silvery light of the moon.

"It's okay," he assured her, "just a flesh wound. I've had worse." Haley gasped.

Frank's eyes softened.

"Your boyfriend wants you real bad, Jenna," Frank's voice was uncompromising yet oddly gentle. "Hitting a safe house, assaulting federal agents and possibly killing U.S. Marshals, he wants you real bad. But I guess he has eight million reasons, doesn't he?"

Haley stared at him. Jenna's boyfriend, Ricky?

Before she could respond, his eyes drew dark. "Someone gave you up, Jenna."

"What do you mean someone gave me up?"

Frank half-smiled. "We didn't even know where you were going to be taken until two hours ago. Someone gave you up."

New fear stripped her senses raw. She stared at Frank, his words still registering but not connecting. Concern for her sister was making her numb with panic.

Glancing at his arm, he said matter-of-factly, "They're

going to be looking for you and I need to get to a hospital. I'll to take where you'll be safe."

Frank pulled his cell phone from his pocket and scrolled down his tiny address book until he found the number he was seeking. Two hits and he held the cell up to his ear.

"Hey Buddy," he said seconds later. "Yeah, hell, I know what time it is, but I'm in real big trouble. I have a package I need you to keep for a few days. Frank took a long breath, the shadows cleared from his eyes. He gave Haley a weak nod as he finally said, "Good, can you meet me at the place where we hooked up last? Great, I'll see you there."

Frank took a long breath. He looked relieved. Turning to her he said, "I have a friend, one I can trust. Hell, at the moment, he's probably the only one I can trust. He'll take care of you for a few days until we get this sorted out."

Haley stood ready with her confession that she wasn't Jenna but the fear she had for her sister had grown tenfold. She couldn't say anything, not just yet. Besides, if Frank knew she was not Jenna, he might very well throw her overboard for the danger she had put them in by not telling him the truth earlier. She held her silence and her secret. The truth or any version of it was not an option. Looking toward the jeweled Miami skyline, Frank restarted the engine and pointed the cigarette toward the southern shore.

"Where are we going?" Haley shouted bracing herself for the Wave Dancer's drive across the ocean.

"To a small marina near Biscayne Bay." He yelled back. "My friend will meet us there."

The deafening grind of the Wave Dancer's engine left little room for conversation. Fearing for his wound, Haley didn't try to distract Frank further. She sat silently suffering the speed boat's repetitive jolts through the Atlantic as the cigarette took wave after jolting wave until they reached the tiny barrier islands just off the coast of Biscayne Bay. Frank slowed the Wave Dancer through the waterway, navigating the boat in almost a clean line toward his destination.

When they reached a small marina filled with boats of varying sizes,, Haley helped Frank secure the boat to the dock. She was grateful they had at last stopped.

"Now what?" Haley asked as Frank secured the last rope to the marina's mooring.

"Now we wait," Frank replied wearily, "and hope I don't die before my friend gets here."

If he had meant to be funny, he had failed. Haley frowned. "We need to call an ambulance." Frank half smiled. "No," his voice was loosing its steely edge. With emphasis, he added, "We stay put. My first priority is keeping you safe."

"Don't be ridiculous," Haley argued. "You've got to get to a doctor before you bleed to death."

Frank chuckled. "Don't worry about me. We've spent years trying penetrating the Rojas Cartel. You're a godsend. We need you alive. Now, I need you to stop arguing with me. My friend should be here shortly."

Seeing Haley's pretty scowl, he added. "Look, sweetie, I appreciate your concern, but we need to sit tight."

Haley leaned back against the seat, hoping whoever 'he' was would hurry. Almost on cue, a dark blue Ford Bronco pulled into the marina and circled the parking lot.

Using the boat's steering wheel as a grip, Frank pulled himself upright and waved. The Bronco made a hairpin turn coming to a full stop directly in front of them.

Haley glimpsed a silhouette of a broad shouldered man dominating the driver's side of the vehicle. The driver sat motionless. Time stopped. A frightening premonition swept over Haley; warning her with a fresh new fear, she couldn't name. Somewhere deep inside her, she knew that from this moment forward, nothing would ever be the same again.

The door opened. A tall man stepped out and headed toward them in a catlike stride. Dressed in a black T-shirt and black jeans, his skin glistened bronze in the moonlight, Haley caught her breath at the broad shoulders. He was menacing and she knew to be afraid. He made no attempt to conceal the restless energy in his muscular physique.

Watching his approach, Haley said under her breath. "This is your friend?"

"That's him," Frank answered with a hard gasp of air.

Stepping under a streetlight, the stranger's short, dark cropped hair glistened in the yellow-white light. A light breeze ruffled one stray lock forward and he swept it back with a large hand.

Haley noted his classically handsome face, his aquiline nose and square jaw. Darkness obscured the color of his eyes. Small drops of moisture clung to his damp forehead and she saw an inherent strength that seemed vaguely familiar.

Hardly giving Haley a glance, he jumped without being asked into the boat. With the craggy look of an unfinished sculpture, he bent his head down to take a better look at Frank's arm. "You didn't tell me you were shot."

"Yeah, well, you can drop me off at the hospital then get out of town. By the way, this is Jenna Rollins. Jenna, this is the infamous Captain Jack Morgan."

With the moonlight against Jack's profile, he stood well over six feet, and possessed a sensuality that was almost frightening. He nodded at her. His generous lips parted to give her a dazzling display of straight white teeth.

Haley stood stupidly, knowing she was the source of

this night's evils. She looked down and away. Men may have died because of Jenna's lies and her silence. She could think of nothing to say that would make up for her duplicity. When she looked back at him, he had already turned from her and was examining Frank Potter's gun shot wound.

"Let's get you to the hospital," Jack snapped.

Without waiting for Frank's reply, he wrapped his powerful arms about Frank and helped him off the boat. Leaving Haley to climb to the dock on her own, the men made their way to the Bronco. Haley scooted around the men and opened the back door of the bronco.

"Try not to get blood all over my seat," Jack said carefully easing his friend into the back seat. Frank's laugh turned into a choking cough.

"I hope you're worth this," Jack growled under his breath toward Haley.

"She's worth it," Frank said catching his breath. "She can bring down the 'Angel de la Morte'."

A cold shiver raced up Haley's arms and choked the breath in her lungs.

Jack's expression tightened.

"The Angel of Death," he translated slowly. "So, she's the one they are looking for?"

Frank nodded and eased across the back of the seat.

"You're one hot little potato." Jack stared at her taking in her long dark hair, her perfectly delicate face and voluptuous body. "I can see why Ricky Rojas wants you back."

"No one must know she's with you," Frank said, "Jack, I need you to keep her safe."

Jack's glance at Haley conveyed his contempt.

"Get in," he snapped at her. Closing Frank's door, he

rounded the back of the Bronco and got in behind the driver's seat.

"Don't you think she'd be safer somewhere else?" Jack asked turning the key in the ignition. "Anywhere else?"

"No," Frank said weakly as they pulled out of the parking lot, "The safe house we had her in was attacked. Someone gave her up. Until we find out who, I need her out of harm's way. She can bring down one of the most vicious drug operations in South Florida."

Haley gasped. Jenna! Oh God, Ricky was involved in drugs? Her mind flashed back to the one time she had met Ricky aboard his yacht. The memory of an exquisite luncheon filled with laughter returned. At the time, all she had seen was Jenna's happiness. It seemed like a fairy tale with her beautiful sister as the princess and Ricky the rich, handsome prince.

Too late, she remembered the two men watching her. The men were not merely Hispanic or Latino, they were Colombian! They were not friends but the bodyguards of a drug lord!

Next to her, Jack looked at Haley noting her paled expression. Served her right, he thought privately, she deserved to be afraid. Glancing back at his friend, he could see Frank was fading fast, too fast. He floored the accelerator, downshifting to increase the Ford's speed. At the moment, he had one thought, to keep Frank Potter alive.

Jack sneered as he pulled onto the main highway. He had little use for those who lived in or around the underbelly of the Miami drug world. This girl, no matter how damn beautiful, was up to her neck in the mire. Sure, he thought running a red light, he could keep her for a few days.

With a sadistic smile, he turned his attention back to the road. She would have little to do but watch the dark ridges of gators glide by his back door. Sand fleas and mosquitoes would bite and sting those beautiful legs. Would she be frightened of the snakes hanging like vines hanging from the mango trees? He wondered if the calls of exotic birds would frighten her in a lost world that time forgot. He wondered if she knew there were things worse than death.

Reaching the newly built hospital at the end of Florida's Turnpike, Jack stopped the Bronco before the sliding emergency room doors. He jumped out of the SUV and hurried to the back passenger's door.

"Keep your head down, Jenna," Frank warned with his breath gasping, "I don't want you seen."

In a softer voice, he added, "Look, I know Jack looks rough around the edges but he's a good guy. You'll be safe. Wait until I contact you. Now lie down, don't let anyone see you."

Haley crouched in the seat. "Thank you," she whispered but the metallic sounds of his door opening covered her words.

Orderlies rushed out of the ER entrance as Jack eased Frank out of the back seat and helped him onto a gurney.

"Take care of the package," Frank pleaded in a weakening voice. "I'll contact you in a few days."

He turned his dulling gaze to the orderlies. "I'm a Federal Marshal. My badge and identification are in my left pocket. I need you to call the U.S. Marshals office in Miami."

Crouched in the seat, Haley heard the shuffle of feet and then the driver door slammed. Without looking up at him, she heard Jack pull away from the emergency room exit.

"You can get up now," he said his voice angry. "You're safe."

"Where are you taking me?" she asked sliding into the seat.

His lips curled into a Machiavellian smile and his handsome face turned into a dark mask of controlled fury. His fingers hardened on the steering wheel as he answered, "To hell."

CHAPTER TWO

The moon once bright began to dim behind multi-layers of thin silvery clouds. The air was still hot, moist and sticky in the South Florida night. Haley looked down the dark alley behind the hospital. It was sheltered on either side by nondescript buildings and bleak hospital annexes.

Exhausted and too afraid to sleep, she wrapped her fingers around the small cell phone in her pocket. She prayed it wouldn't need recharging before Jenna's promised call. The slick little metal cell was her lifeline to Jenna and what was left of humanity this night.

With a sideways glance at Jack Morgan, she was annoyed to find him grinning at her. If his intention was to frighten her, he had. Taking a deep breath, she tried to steady her nerves and focus her on anything else but their ultimate destination and the dark companion taking her there.

She had felt some measure of safety with Frank Porter. Frank. It was good to worry about someone else besides Jenna or herself. Frank's wound did not appear to be, to her untrained eye, life threatening and she was grateful he was receiving medical attention but she remembered the other agents and shuttered. Guilt washed over her. Was her life more important than the lives of the men who had died defending her? Consumed by regret, she knew she had to tell Frank the truth. He would be angry but surely he, the government, would help.

Dismissing the desperate image of that inevitable future,

she brought her attention back to the moment. Tonight there was no need to tell Frank or any one else who she was. Jenna would resurface with a good explanation. Her twin would be in the safe custody of the U.S. Marshals, and she would return to her unassuming little existence at Vero Beach's quiet little book store.

She brought her hand from her pocket so as not to draw attention to the cell phone hidden there then folded her hands in her lap. They looked awkward. She reached for her purse and clutched it too tightly. Stealing a quick glance at the man next to her, she was grateful to find his attention was on the road.

With a new sense of urgency, she once again began searching for a street sign, a post office or business name, anything that would hint of their location. She needed to know where they were.

The sweltering night heat told her they were far south of the gold coast cities of Miami and Fort Lauderdale. Frank had brought the cigarette in at the breakneck speed toward the dark shoreline. Her memory of their ride consisted of dark choppy waters, the sparkling lights of the south coast and the diminutive barrier islands that Frank smoothly scooted around. He knew the route to the marina, for which Haley was grateful.

With only bobbing channel markers to guide them, they at last reached a small, over- crowded marina. The short ride to the hospital revealed nothing except road signs to direct traffic toward the turnpike. She could be anywhere. She needed to know where.

Desperate to find a point of reference, she read several small businesses named after their owner or products. At that moment, she looked out the window to see an oversized green neon sign atop a small block building. It read Homestead Tool and Hardware. Feeling her body relax, a small sigh slipped from her lips. They were not on route to hell. They were in Homestead, Florida, Gateway to the Florida Keys. Settling back into the seat, this small bit of information gave her some sense of bearing.

Frank had brought the Wave Dancer further south than she had first suspected. They must have docked at Biscayne Marina. She was in Homestead, a small town made famous by Hurricane Andrew's devastating path in 1995. Knowing where they were calmed her. If she had to get away from Jack Morgan, she could find her way home.

The only traffic at this hour was long bed produce trucks and small cars hurrying to make the early morning run to Miami some 35 miles away.

Jack eased the Bronco off the dark four lane highway toward a directional sign that read Florida City. They were not headed south toward the Keys but west. He was taking her into the 'glades.

Why would he be taking her into the Everglades? Images began building in her mind. Biting her lip she turned away. With crime on the rise in South Florida, one too many bodies were turning up in the 'glades. Would she be next?

Frank had asked Jack to keep her safe. She corrected herself; Frank had asked Jack to keep Jenna safe. She wasn't Jenna. Trying to steady her nerves, she drew a quiet breath and wondered how long before they realized she wasn't her sister.

The homes and businesses outside Florida City grew increasingly infrequent with each passing mile.

She had to know more about Jack Morgan. She looked at him and softly asked, "Are you a U.S. Marshall or FBI Agent?"

"Neither, Sweetie," Jack answered in a voice as soft as velvet, "I'm in the witness protection program. Welcome to the club."

Suddenly she understood. Jenna had run from Ricky to Federal Marshals for protection. This would have been a good thing had Jenna not traded places with her. Haley sat silent as Jon drove past small frame farm houses with chain link fences. Only Floridians knew it was not to keep the house pets in but the gators out.

Passing an endless grove of orange and grapefruit trees, she was so lost in thought; she scarcely noticed when Jack turned off the main road to a smaller artery. Several miles from the turn off she read the Welcome sign to Florida Everglades.

Driving into the park they passed the Visitor Center where she and Jenna had visited on a school trip. She still recalled the tour guide telling them that the Everglades were more than just sawgrass but a subtropical wilderness filled with pine forest, hardwood hammocks, royal palms, cypress swamps and mangroves.

The Indians had called this place the river of grass but she could see nothing now as the moon had slipped from the horizon. Murky pitch blanketed the Everglades hiding the sultry scenery and its exotic abundance of wildlife. This was gator country. They slithered and sunned on miry banks as ancient sentinels guarding their habitat from the constant invasion of man. Though their numbers were on the rise, their battle for land was sadly predestined.

With morning hours away, the air was clean, fresh and filled with a soft mixture of fragrant sweet flowers.

For a moment, Haley wondered once again if she should tell Jack Morgan she was not Jenna but her twin, but she knew she couldn't, not without endangering Jenna's life more. She couldn't trust him with her secret or with her life.

She could play along with this forced masquerade for a couple of days; she vowed looking out at the primeval land filled with tall pines and dwarf cypress. She shot him a withering glance. She needed to know more about Jack Morgan.

She let an anxious little cough cover her nervousness. "You said you heard someone was looking for me?"

Jack laughed. "Yeah, half of Florida. Your boyfriend, Ricky Rojas has put a bounty on you."

Across from her, Jack almost laughed when he saw her look of surprise. She paled and her body was shaking. Something about her reaction wasn't right. He could feel it.

Throughout the ride, Jack tried to ignore the sexy little brunette seated next to him. Try as he could, there was no escaping the melodious softness in her voice or even each sensuous breath that escaped her perfectly formed mouth. Under different circumstances, he would have liked to kiss those lips. Her luminous blue eyes were wide, frightened and hid a secret he wanted to know.

His fingers tightened around the steering wheel as he noted the uneven rise and fall of her full breasts against her blouse. The short skirt she wore was simple and he caught his breath as she slid one beautiful thigh over the other. Each uneasy gesture told him she was lying. About what?

Her beautifully sculptured hands were twisting nervously in her lap. He guessed she was hiding something in the pockets of her small skirt. What? No, a gun would be more pronounced. He pretended not to notice but he knew she carried something of value there.

With an arched brow, he took note of her well defined

arms. She worked out. So, he thought with a wry smile, South Beach Party girls did raise more than a martini glass.

He was filled with curious longing as he continued to watch her. Her eyes fill with quiet contemplation. What was she thinking or planning? Was she involved in the attack on the Marshals? Had she surrendered herself to them or had she been taken into custody?

He considered leaving her alone on this desolate stretch of highway but he knew he wouldn't. He tired to tell himself it was because of his promise to Frank but he knew he would never leave her vulnerable to any kind of predators.

He steadied his hand on the wheel. Unable to shake the feeling that she was either hiding something or something was frightening her, he decided he needed to know more about Miss Jenna Rollins and her secrets. Both their lives might depend on it.

He drove past the signs of Pa-hay-okee, Mahogany Hammock and Paurotis Pond. They'd be in Flamingo soon before they reached their final destination, Pirates Cove. He doubted she would like it there any more than the pirates and buccaneers who had been marooned there centuries before.

"How exactly did Frank get shot?" His words were as cool and clear as ice water.

"Protecting me," came Haley's honest reply. Her breath burned in her throat. "He was protecting me."

Jack kept his attention on the road and saw a small Florida panther dart across the road jumping the headlights as if they were obstacles thrown in his path.

"Tell me what happened tonight?"

Haley stared out into the darkness and brushed a long thick lock of hair from her face. She began slowly and measured each word. "The Marshals picked me up at a motel and took me to a safe house. I went out to the balcony to get a bit of fresh air when I saw a group of gunman headed toward the house. There was a gun battle."

She grew stilled and serious. Shifting slightly, she continued. "The agents held their ground, protecting me. Frank pulled me out of the house, in the boat. He called you when we stopped. I didn't even realize he had been shot until we were out in the Gulf Stream."

Jack sat quietly. Who had given her up? The locations of 'Safe Houses' were kept classified. So, he concluded, that's why Frank had called him. No one would ever suspect Ricky Rojas's South Beach Princess was hiding in the hell hole he called home? Who would see her or know she was there? The irony of his existence was not lost on him. He wanted to know more about her.

"I guess you can't or won't tell me more," he asked in a voice that was tense and chipped with bitterness.

"I can't," Haley answered. There was nothing more she could tell.

A cold knot formed in her stomach; whatever or whoever he was, he was her only salvation. Haley had no choice but to trust Jack, if not with the truth, then with her life. In a voice so soft she wasn't sure he heard her, she said, "Thank you for taking me in."

"I owe Frank," Jack explained, and his voice carried a silken thread of warning. It was late. He was worried about Frank and unnerved by the wisp of femininity seated beside him. "Frank took a bullet meant to kill me. I owe him my life, Jenna and I promised to keep you safe. Safe you will be."

Haley sat quietly, it was still critical she learn more about him. Finally she nerved to ask, "You said you were in the Witness Protection Program, are you a…"

"Hit man?" Jack finished for her. He watched her face color and laughed. "No, I'm not a hit man, a snitch or a mobster. A few years back, I witnessed a mob hit in Vegas. I did the right thing, I testified against the shooter. He's in Club Fed and I'm running a bait shop, bar and boat rental in the Everglades."

Haley sat silent. She heard the bitterness in Jack's voice as he spat out his story. She shifted nervously in her seat.

"I'm sorry to inconvenience you," she apologized. Suddenly she realized Jack might not be the only one inconvenienced by her arrival. "Will your wife mind?"

"No wife, Sweetie, just you and me, the gators, snakes and a few fishermen," Jack answered steering the SUV through a broken orange crate scatted across the road. Changing the subject, he asked, "So how did you meet the Angel of Death?"

"Don't call him that," Haley snapped but not for the reasons he would suspect. She couldn't bear to think Jenna was being pursued by a vicious drug lord.

"How much do you know about your boyfriend?"

"I didn't know he was involved in drugs," came her quick reply.

Jack snorted. "I don't believe you. Where exactly did you think he got his money?"

Haley angrily crossed her arms; Jack Morgan who knew nothing about her or her sister.

"What time is it?" Haley asked changing the subject.

"It's close to four," Jack answered. "We'll be there shortly."

True to his word, less than ten minutes later, they drove into Flamingo and its tiny marina on Florida Bay.

It was August and the sand flees and mosquitoes were

thick. The temperatures were unbearable. No one came to visit except for a few diehard fishermen. No one stayed long.

Passing through Flamingo, Jack drove across a small bridge built by the Army Core of Engineers in the 1920's. He leaned back against the seat grateful to be home. He suddenly found it odd to consider this home. His bait shop and bar was the only business on a tiny stretch of land known as Pirates Cove and he should be grateful that it was a long-time favorite with fishermen.

On occasion he rented boats to European tourists or to newlyweds who wanted to experience the Everglades and knew nothing about the luxurious hotels scattered along the Florida Keys. Once they learned; they never came back.

Beside him, Haley sat quietly. Driving over the small bridge, the bronco's high beams flashed on a small welcome sign that showed visitors the way to Pirates Cove. She heard the sounds of water lapping the shore but could see nothing in the dark.

Jack stopped the bronco before a small rustic shack. The sign above the door read, Capt. Jack's Bait and Tackle. He was Captain Jack, Haley thought, and they were indeed at the end of the world.

CHAPTER THREE

How did you ever find this place?" Haley asked.

The bitterness of Jack's laugh cut through the night air.

"It may surprise you to know that once I was General Manager of a Las Vegas hotel and casino. I had it all. The witness protection makes every attempt to find something that they consider similar to your career. This was someone's idea of a resort."

Jack got out of the bronco and stretched his long legs. Haley, likewise, slid out of the passenger seat. Her feet were instantly attacked by sand fleas. Two motion detector lights illuminated the darkness. The closest to the bronco lit the small parking lot. The second light lit a small boat launch where she saw a rack of canoes, several John boats and the frame of an Airboat.

An unsettling quiet wrapped them like a blanket and muffled the sounds of their feet as they walked toward the front door. If her logistics were correct, Key West and the lower Keys would be directly south from their location and the Dry Tortugas to their west. The back of the Bait Shop hid a spectacular panorama of Florida Bay and the Gulf of Mexico. It was a small thing to look forward to tomorrow.

"Come on," Jack urged her as he walked to the wooden porch. "Get in before the sand fleas eat you alive."

Taking his advice, Haley hurried toward the screen door.

Jack held the door open for her, and then left her standing at the entryway while he moved quickly through the dark room. She heard the plastic snap of a light switch and the room was instantly filled with fluorescent light.

A lacquered bar ran from almost one end of the room to the other. Empty bar stools stood as the last visitor had left them. A large pool table dominated the far end of the room and to her left stood several commercial refrigerators. Through the glass doors, she gave a fleeting look at the brands of beer and variety of frozen bait displayed there. Haley cringed. Testosterone haunted every corner of the empty bar. The only thing missing was a cheeky pin-up calendar. Several wooden tables with chairs rested in the middle of the room; Jack motioned for her to sit at one of them.

Walking behind the bar, Jack asked, "Are you hungry? Thirsty?"

His handsome face was reserved, rugged and somber against his tanned skin. His arresting good looks captured her attention. Her breath quickened and she felt a blush burn her cheeks. She turned away, feigning interest in a newspaper clipping of a fisherman beside a shark strung from lift. With a small cough, she said softly, "If you don't mind, I'd like a diet soda."

"A diet soda," he repeated with a half grim. There was something lazy and seductive in his manner as he rolled a cooler's lid back. She heard the metallic sound of cans shifting about before he snapped the cooler shut. "We don't get much call for diet drinks here but you're in luck."

Pulling a bottle of hard whiskey out from behind the bar, he grabbed a shot glass and returned to her. Offering her the diet soda, he then poured himself a shot. He tipped the glass slightly and swirled the dark alcohol about before taking a small sip. He placed the shot glass down in front of him and said to her, "You're a long way from South Beach, honey."

His deep voice simmered with checked control. He waited, challenging her with his eyes.

Haley took a sip of her drink. For the time being she was Jenna, until she could be Haley again and her sister was safe, he could think what he liked.

"Can I fix your something to eat?" He offered slowly, "I've got hamburgers, steak, bacon and eggs?"

"No thank you," she answered swallowing hard, "I'm not hungry but thanks for the offer."

Across from her, Jack downed his whiskey. Again she noticed the way his powerful chest strained against the fabric of the black T-shirt he wore. His stare was relentless in fevered passion as his eyes swept over her face, her lips and her hair.

He relaxed with one leg stretched out before him, the other neatly tucked under the table. The black denim of his jeans clung to his thighs like a second skin. She could sense the controlled power coiled in his body. He was a predator.

Haley tried to focus her attention on anything away from his utterly masculine body but it was impossible to ignore the seductive heat of his dark brown eyes. Drops of moisture clung to his damp forehead and his lips opened slowly as he took slow sip of the whiskey. His fingers sensually played with the rim of the glass, making her heart hammer foolishly.

She swallowed hard and pretended not to notice the magnetism that was building between them. Taking a sip of diet Coke, her mouth spread into a thin-lipped smile which he politely ignored.

"You know," he began lazily, glancing around the bar, "there was a time I oversaw the operation of a 500 seat restaurant in my casino. Now, I can mange this."

"You sound so bitter," Haley said, hopeful he would tell her more. His brow dipped into a deeper frown.

"Yeah, I suppose I am," Jack stated flatly, "but I'm not mad at the federal government. I'm mad that they took my livelihood, my career and my life."

"But you're safe," came Haley's response. Anger flashed in his dark eyes and she regretted her words and tried to make up for her error. "Well, can't they find you another 'place' if you are unhappy here? Won't they underwrite your income until you do?"

Jack scowled. "They help for about three months, sugar. Then you're on your own. What sort of job do you do?"

"I'm a model," Haley lied. At least Jenna was. She shuttered and thought of her job at the bookstore for the first time since arriving in South Florida.

She would somehow have to make a call and an excuse for Joanne, the bookstore owner. Thank goodness business was light this time of year and she hadn't taken a vacation in years. She didn't think it would be a problem but the short notice would. She would have to deal with it in the morning.

Unable to contain a yawn, she covered her mouth. She was exhausted and needed rest. Her attraction to this man was taking her soul to places she should never go, especially with him. After all, she had her sister to think about and the next lie she would be expected to tell. The sensual intimacy of the moment was robbing her of logic and reason. She was tired; she wanted to go to bed.

"If you don't mind," she said finishing the last of her soda, "I need to lie down. Thank you for the soda."

He took a last swig of his whiskey and rose to his feet. "Follow me."

Without saying another word, Haley followed him through

the kitchen to a closed door marked private. On the other side she was astonished to find an enormous living room with a front wall made up of sliding glass doors and heavy windows that stretched from the ceiling to the floor. The seascape of the Gulf of Mexico and Florida Bay would be breathtaking in the light of day.

In contrast to the restaurant's rustic interior, Jack's private living quarters were lavish and smart. Heavy comfortable furniture rested on a beautiful hard wood floor. In one corner of the room sat his computer workstation.

"That's where I plan to write my great American novel," he said motioning toward the computer. He sounded disinterested and unattached. What must it be like to lose everything?

She felt sad for him. What was it like to live without hope? "Do you really want to write a great American novel?"

Jack glared at her. "No. I want to have my life back."

There was no end of his bitterness. With a quick glance around the living area, Haley said, "This room is magnificent."

White ceiling fans spun in steady rhythm. The two oversized chairs and sofa were beige with a light green palm pattern. The end tables and coffee table were a rich golden teak.

Several oil paintings hung on the back wall and the rest of the wall space was covered in book shelves overflowing with books. Haley smiled. Perhaps, she could find a common ground with this man after all.

Jack watched her take in his living room. Compared to the restaurant, it took most people by surprise. Careful to keep emotion out of his face, he was pleased to see her skimming the titles of his books.

It was good to see his world through her eyes. Though

still suspicious of her, he grudgingly acknowledged having a pretty girl around for a few days would be a welcome treat from the weathered fisherman who came in to drink beer.

Walking to the far end of the room, he swung open the door to his guest room.

"You can stay here," he said. His eyes were dark and smoldering like summer lighting. "I don't know about the sheets but they're clean. I haven't had any visitors except for Frank a couple of months back."

Haley nodded. There was a doe like quality about her that tugged at his heart strings. God was she beautiful, he thought as she walked into the room and sat on the edge of the bed.

"There might be a shirt in the closet if you need something to wear. By the way, we'll be sharing a bathroom."

"Thank you," Haley said softly looking about the simple yet elegant guest room.

For a moment he lingered at the door, once again taking in every inch of her small frame. "If you need anything just call. The walls are paper thin and I sleep with one eye open. Have for a long time."

Haley nodded. "Goodnight."

"Goodnight," he repeated gently closing the door. With a frown he left her, not wanting to go. She was in his care. She was hands off. She belonged to Ricky Rojas.

God he wanted to touch those soft lips and cup those supple breasts, but he couldn't. He wouldn't. He shrugged. It was none of his business and she would be out of his life in a few days.

Right now he needed to think about something besides that hot sexy little body in the next room. He needed a shower; instead, he went outside for a cigarette.

"Damn it," Jack said as he took his first drag. He had

given cigarettes up five months ago, now he held the cancer stick between his fingers.

In the dark, he heard the sound of an animal moving about the edge of his yard. Otter, raccoon, possum, he thought taking a drag.

What the hell had he gotten into; he thought to himself. He remembered the way her mouth sensually moved when she spoke, the sweet sound of her voice, and the soft blue of her eyes and voluptuous curves of her body. Was she as innocent as she looked? No one could be that innocent.

The cigarette tasted bitter to him and he tossed it to his feet. It had been too dry and there was a Fire Alert in the 'glades. He took care to burn into to the earth. He didn't care about much these days but a few wild animals who shared space with him on Pirates Cove. In his own fashion, he had become an environmentalist for this lost world.

Taking a long breath, he couldn't help but think of the sensual Ms. Rollins. She looked like the girl next door but he knew her type. Women like her hung on the arms of fat, balding winners at a Vegas craps table. They spent every dime they had on designer clothes, make-up and hair and had hearts harder than the diamonds they coveted. Vegas or South Beach, these women went through men like last season's designer clothes always looking for one brighter and more expensive.

At the top of his game, he had made a career of steering clear of woman like her and yet thinking of her now, he had no doubt her full length of thick hair would be soft to his fingers. He remembered the curves of her full lips, the silky smooth lines of her neck and the fragile way her fingers moved. He wondered how she would feel moving under him. He understood how Ricky Rojas would want her back; if he had her, he'd want her back.

He felt hot and sticky and his clothes were melting into his body. A shower would be good. A cold one!

In the room he threw his clothes into a heap on the floor. Cursing his thoughts and his needs, he racked his hand unceremoniously through his short dark hair and grabbed for the bathroom door knob.

Jerking open the door, thick white steam curled about him. Overhead lights hit him square in the face.

Haley screamed in surprise. She made a feeble attempt of hiding her breasts which were lathered in white foaming soap.

"Sorry," Jack said, but instead of stepping gallantly out of the bathroom, he stood breathless, taking in every inch of her voluptuous body.

As their eyes locked, Haley took a quick breath and stared at him in astonishment.

"Get out!" she screamed above the flow of water.

Jack grinned. "I said I'm sorry."

"You don't look it," Haley snapped. She felt a hot blush burn her face as he continued in his slow cool appraisal of her body.

His warm brown eyes traveled from her face to her shoulder to her breasts.

Jack stood helpless to turn away from her; his eyes moved slowly from her full breasts to her flat tummy, before examining her long silky legs. God, how he would like to explore those rosy nipples with his tongue.

The smoldering flame in his eyes disarmed her and stripped her raw.

Across from him, she was unable to turn away from his brawny chest, powerful arms and shoulders, his flat abdomen, the hardening masculinity and sculptured thighs and calves.

His gaze burned through her. At last he looked away. "I should have knocked."

"It's okay," she stammered, embarrassed and perplexed by her own intensity at the site of him. "Just please, please leave."

He nodded and left the bath. Haley leaned into the shower, bracing her hands against the tile. Fighting back tears and exhaustion, she gathered what strength she had, turned off the water and grabbed for the towel and her clothes before quickly leaving the room.

Snapping off the light in the guest room, she slipped under the covers, embarrassed and angry at herself and him. She wallowed deep into the mattress. She lay breathless, afraid he would follow her and knowing all the while she wanted him to come.

In the darkness, she felt her face burn.

The encounter had left her senses reeling. Her heart was pounding with feelings and emotions she had thought long dead. It was all too much she thought blinking away tears that burned her eyes. Trying to slow her heart, she struggled to pull together the last hours of her life. She reached across to the night stand and grasped the little cell. It was her lifeline to Jenna. She fell asleep only to dream of men chasing her before she fell into the arms of a pirate.

In his own room Jack took a deep breath. He hadn't expected to find his beautiful house guest naked in the shower and finding her there he had been captivated, unable to move, unable to breathe.

He had gone in there to take away his need of her now he was consumed by it. He wanted to ravage her body until he was lost in her arms. He knew her skin would be like velvet to his touch. Her lips would taste like honey. Her soft smile was a siren's call and he was powerless to resist. His need of this woman was making him senseless.

He saw the bathroom light go out from under the door and heard the slow closing of a door. She had left the bathroom and was in her bed.

Thoughts of her lying there were leaving him weak. He retuned to the bathroom and found it extraordinary void without her little presence.

Turning on the shower, he stepped into the cool spray of water and acknowledged he had been too damn long without a woman. Scrubbing his body, he allowed the water to cool his desires as he reminded himself she belonged or at least was wanted by the most vicious drug lord in South Florida. He already had a contract on him for testifying on Vinnie the Rat; he didn't need the Angel de la Morte hunting him down, too.

The cold water was not working. Some twenty minutes later, he was in his own bed, with more questions than answers. He lay for a long time staring into the darkness. She was the one woman he could never touch and he wanted her badly.

Feeling his body drift to sleep, he hoped to hell Frank found another place for her soon and he hoped to hell he wouldn't follow her there.

CHAPTER FOUR

A gunshot blast woke Jack. Bolting upright, he reached to his nightstand and jerked open the top drawer. The cold handle of his Sig Saur was firmly in his grasp, his finger poised on the trigger, before he checked himself. He had been dreaming. Again.

His heart was racing and his body was dripping wet with sweat. He returned the gun to the drawer.

Outside his bedroom window he could see a white heron walking gracefully at the water's edge. The heron's full attention was on the minnows and insects swarming by the bank. It dropped its elegant white neck and retrieved a small fish before downing his treat in a single swallow. No gunshot had disturbed the morning quiet.

He fell back against his pillows and tried to steady his breath. Reminding himself it was just another day in paradise.

It had been months since the dream had visited him and it was always the same.

It was Vinnie Giavannelli, commonly known as Vinnie the Rat, holding a gun on him. He saw the white explosion at the tip of Vinnie's handgun, heard the blast like rolling thunder and watched as the bullet moved toward him in slow motion. He counted his life in seconds.

In his dream, Frank wasn't there to save him. In his dream, he was always alone. It was only then he remembered his houseguest. It was almost eleven-thirty.

Cursing the hour, he threw back the covers wondering if she had taken off with his SUV. It would serve him right, he thought, sliding into a pair of jeans.

Barefoot and bare chest, he jerked open the bedroom door expecting the worse of Jenna Rollins just in time to see his beautiful house guest walking into the living room with a platter of golden brown biscuits.

She smiled at him.

His eyes followed the soft sway of her hips as she moved quietly through the living room to the sliding glass doors then out to the wooden deck that over looked Florida Bay.

In the morning sun her long brown hair shimmered in thick heavenly waves and carelessly tumbled down her back. It glistened with auburn streaks. Her full breasts pushed against her blouse and the short skirt she wore accented her small waist, shapely hips and soft round bottom. He watched as her bare feet arched prettily as she placed the biscuits in the center of the table. The strain on her calves emphasized neat little toned muscles and silken thighs. She was seductive, sexy and didn't even know it.

Looking over her shoulder, she said, "Good Morning. I hope you don't mind, but I was hungry and made us some breakfast."

"Hell no," Jack said looking at the table. Every inch of the small table was crowded with eggs, hash browns, ham, bacon and biscuits. Somehow she had found the stoneware he rarely used and he didn't even know he had a small coffee service.

Her long thick lashes swept down across her cheekbones and he remembered her from the night before trying to cover her firm high perched breasts while sudsy white soap cascaded about her flat stomach and down her pretty legs.

She looked up to him and smiled. He couldn't help but

wonder if her wide-eyed innocence was just another smoke screen. If it was, she played her part well. Why the hell did she have to be so damn beautiful, he cursed inwardly? And why the hell did she have to belong to someone else. If wishes were horses, he thought returning to his room.

Grabbing a clean shirt from the closet, he acknowledged the mire of conflicting emotions, and he needed to remind himself she was no angel. Jenna Rollins was up to her pretty little ass in drugs and a medley of street crime. She was probably very good at what she does, he thought refusing to believe what his senses were hammering home.

He had expected her gone. He had anticipated she would be expecting to be carefully kept by him; a pampered little rich girl with endless demands. Instead, she had made breakfast and managed to look fresh, innocent and so unlike the party girl reputation circulating South Florida. Whatever she was, he told himself, she wasn't what she seemed and she was the last thing he needed.

"You've been too long without a woman, pal," he said allowing his voice to harden. "Get a grip. You've got a contract on you by the Ragazzo Mob; you don't need the Columbians after you, too."

He had a cool head by the time he retuned to her. Except for a few beers, this was the first time the table had seen food. She had even managed to find small flowers and placed them in a rock glass in its center.

She smiled sweetly at him, picked up her napkin and laid it in her lap. Giving him a doe-eyed look, she reached for a biscuit and said, "Bon Appetite."

"This is new," Jack said with some measure of appreciation. He pulled back his chair and sat already reaching for a plate of bacon and eggs. Though she was dressed in the same outfit she had worn the night before she managed to look as fresh as the tiny wildflowers she had gathered for the centerpiece.

"I'm used to getting up early," Haley said buttering her biscuit. With a shy smile, she decided not to tell him she opened the bookstore up at six am every morning so shoppers could purchase the morning edition of the Times News.

Returning her attention to her hunger, she scooped up some scrambled eggs, a small piece of ham and a single bacon strip. She tried to concentrate on her breakfast but it was impossible to ignore the smooth powerful chest beneath his open shirt. His face in the morning light was bronzed by wind and sun. His lips were firm, full and smooth. His short dark hair framed his handsome face and the shadows of his beard provided a sensual contrast to his polished veneer. There was a smoldering fire in his dark brown eyes and Haley wondered what it would be like to be wanted by such a man. She would never know, she thought, taking a bit of egg.

Too quick, she remembered him standing naked in the bathroom last night and was acutely conscious of his rock hard body chiseled in perfect proportions.

"It's been a long time since anyone has bothered to fix me breakfast," he said thankfully breaking into her thoughts. He picked up and examined one of the biscuits. "Are these homemade?"

"Yes," Haley replied realizing she had left the butter in the kitchen. "Oh, I forgot to bring the butter out. I'll be right back."

Jack reached up and gently cuffed her wrists sending electric shocks through her. She froze and waited for him to speak.

"These don't need butter, Jenna. They're delicious." Jack

said as he released her wrist. His mouth curled into a devastating grin. "I didn't know you party girls knew how to cook."

Haley straightened her shoulders. "I told you before I'm no party girl."

Raising a fine arched eyebrow, Jack was beginning to suspect she was right. The dots weren't connecting.

"I appreciate you letting me stay here." Haley said politely. "But I don't want you or anyone else to feel obligated to..."

Jack stopped eating and looked at her.

"Don't worry about it. I have a string of fugitives in and out of here al the time," his voice rich with sarcasm. Seeing her frown, he added, "Look, you keep cooking like this, I may hire you on."

Ignoring his off-handed compliment, Haley returned to her breakfast and paid little heed to the blush spreading across her face. It had been a long time since she had gotten a flattering remark, especially from so handsome a man.

"We'll have to get you some clothes today," Jack said taking a big slice of ham.

Haley glanced down at her wrinkled clothes. She needed something fresh to wear. She gave him a weak nod.

Finished with his breakfast, Jack pushed his plate aside. "They have a few things at the marina in Flamingo. We'll go there after we eat."

"That would be great," she said softly and enjoyed the last bits of hash browns on her plate.

In no rush, she sipped her coffee, her thoughts returning to Jenna. Where was she? She still couldn't believe Ricky was a drug dealer, maybe more. How had Jenna gotten involved in him?

She lay in the bed that morning until restless energy and her own hunger urged her into the kitchen. She had gone into the kitchen to make coffee, and then busied herself with preparing their breakfast; anything to keep busy as she willed the cell phone to ring.

Across from her the blue waters of Florida Bay glistened with shiny specks of sunlight. A flock of brown Pelicans glided on top of the indigo sea before vanishing into dark outlines on the distant horizon.

Across from her, Jack was silent. Though he seemed grudgingly cordial this morning, she still remembered his stinging bites from the night before. Taking another sip of coffee, she realized she might very well need this man's amity if not his friendship in the next several days. She had to find a way to cross the bridge between them and climb the wall he had carefully built around himself.

Watching him she realized how different his life must have been before he had testified for the federal government. What would his life have been like now if he hadn't? Was his life of isolation all so different from hers? Jack's seclusion had been forced while hers had been voluntary. Jack wanted life, she had hid from it. They were so different and yet fate had made them very much alike.

Why had she hid herself? Because, she was the responsible one, the good girl perhaps, to balance to Jenna's wild and wanton nature. She gathered her drifting thoughts together vowing she could ill afford self pity now while Jenna's life was in danger.

It was at that moment that Jack's cell phone rang. He pulled it out of his pocket and said hello. After a pause, his face relaxed.

"So you're alive," he said to the caller. He looked at Haley and mouthed the name Frank. He nodded. "Yes, your package is safe."

He paused listening to what was being said. "I understand. I'll talk to you then."

Laying the cell phone on the table beside him and looking at Haley he said, "Frank's gonna be okay."

Relief swept over her.

"He's convinced that someone within the Marshals' office gave away your location but he has no idea who. They're trying to make safer arrangements but I'm afraid you are stuck here for a few days."

Haley stared wordless across from him, her heart pounding. A few days! I can't stay here for a few days; she wanted to scream at him. I have to find my sister!

Jack rose and gathered the silverware onto his plate.

"I'll take care of the dishes," Haley said grabbing the empty egg platter.

"The dishes can wait," Jack said firmly. "I'll get them into the kitchen; go get your shoes on; we'll run over there and see what they have. Look, Jenna, we don't know what will happen in the next few days. Its best we be prepared."

He had said 'we,' Haley realized, feeling for the moment less alone.

"So, go wash your hands, powder your nose or do what you ladies do. I'll be ready to leave when you return."

With a nod, Haley returned to the privacy of the guest room. She pulled Jenna's cell phone out of her pocket and dialed Vero Beach. She had to risk calling Joanne. She should have called earlier.

"Joanne's Book Nook," her boss brightly answered the call.

"Joanne," Haley apologized, "I'm so sorry but there's been an emergency, Jenna is in real trouble and I need to take off a few days."

"Of course, Haley, you have accumulated more sick days than Carter has pills. Anything I can do?"

"No, but I promise to call in a few days. I'm so sorry."

"Honey lamb, it's pretty slow right now. Gail has been asking for more time, so it won't be a problem. Just take care and hurry back."

"I will," Haley promised ending the call. Gail. Gail wanted her job. Haley took a deep breath; maybe she should have it. Maybe it was time for her to move on with her life.

She gave the cell a quick glance and saw there was still time left on the charge. It wouldn't last long; she had to find a way to keep it charged. She was going to have to trust Jack and she wasn't at all sure she could. She had to find Jenna.

"Ready?" Jack asked with a sharp rap at the door.

"Yes," Haley replied tucking the cell deep within her pocket. She grabbed her purse and followed him out to his SUV.

Jack said the marina's tourist shop offered little clothing and he told the truth. Haley managed to pick out a pair of bright pink shorts that were too short, three T-Shirts that said 'I love Florida' and a small floral sun dress. Satisfied this would get her through the next several days, she laid her choices in front of the cashier.

Jack walked up behind her and dropped down a pair of sun glasses and a baseball cap atop the clothing. "You might want these."

Haley nodded. "Good idea."

Pulling her credit card out of her wallet, Jack covered her hand.

"You can't use it, honey. Let me pay. You can reimburse me later."

Haley's mouth went dry. She froze realizing she had almost

laid down a credit card that read Haley M. Rollins. Would he have noticed? She shuttered understanding the consequence her thoughtless act could have caused her.

She saw the twitch of concern in Jack's eyes and guessed he was thinking of Ricky Rojas. If his people had found out where the Safe House was, they might be watching Jenna's credit cards as well. Jack had been quick thinking; she had not and might have risked exposure and maybe her sister's life.

"Thank you," she said softly. Her fingers were shaking as she slipped the master card back into her wallet. She was surprised to find a faraway look of tenderness in his warm brown eyes. She was struck with the knowledge that despite his harsh words, he had taken her in, he was keeping her safe. He was a good man.

Laying cash out on the countertop, he said to her, "Don't worry, this won't set me back too far."

Nervous energy made her laugh. Headed back to Pirates Cove minutes later she donned the baseball cap and sunglasses.

"How do I look?" she asked feeling cheery.

"Cute as hell," Jack said with a grin and an admiring glance in her direction. He had to remind himself that she wasn't his date; he was keeping her safe, that's all. She would be gone soon enough. Don't flirt with her; he warned himself, she's not for you. All the while he knew he was becoming lost in her blue eyes, her soft smile and each inviting curve of her body.

Pirates Cove was less than a mile from the marina and he drove home far too fast. What are you running from? He asked himself. What are you running to?

Haley took her purchases to the guest room when they arrived back at his house and laid her clothes on top the bed.

Haley made another anxious check of the cell phone. It was almost dead. She had no choice. She was going to have to ask Jack for help.

Changing into the little yellow sundress, she found him in the living room at his computer checking his email.

Taking a deep breath, she moved slowly to his side and swallowed hard. Lifting her chin to meet his eyes, she asked. "Do you have a cell phone charger?"

Jack stared at her. The camaraderie they shared only moments earlier was gone. She watched as his eyes turned cold.

"Do you need one?" he asked his voice as cool as ice water.

"Yes," she said forbidding herself to tremble, "I'm expecting a call from my sister."

"You know that's out of the question. You can have no contact with anyone, especially a family member."

His voice was angry and bitter.

Girding herself with resolve, she fought hard against the tears she refused to let fall. She drew a deep breath and forbade herself to tremble. What if he took the phone from her? She clutched it tighter. She had to keep the phone charged! It was her lifeline to Jenna!

"Do you or don't you have a charger?" she demanded.

Jack leaned back in his chair. His brown eyes narrowed speculatively. Her request was simple enough but it carried with it deadly consequences. He doubted Frank, the Marshals or the FBI knew she had the phone on her. They should have checked.

"Who are you planning to call?" his voice was low and smooth. "Ricky?"

"Of course not," Haley spat. "But I need to keep this line open for my sister."

"Why?"

She turned her head away and it was at that moment, Jack suspected the cell phone and her sister were part of the secret she was keeping from him.

"I can't tell you why," Haley began miserably looking back at him, "but I can promise you, I won't be contacting Ricky or anyone else that will put you in danger."

Jack jumped to his feet. "Me? Do you think this is about me, Jenna? Frank is lying in the hospital. Two agents were killed last night and one is in critical care. Do you think this is a game, party girl?"

Haley grasped. Two men were dead because of her.

Jack continued his assault. "You got yourself mixed up with a Columbian Drug Lord who's turning south Florida inside out trying to find you. They'll kill you when they find you, little girl. Get this, Ricky Rojas wants you dead!"

Frightened for Jenna, sickened at her involvement, she clutched the back of the couch for support. "I'm so sorry, I didn't know," she sobbed. Looking back up to him, her body trembling, she could manage no more than a whisper when she said firmly, "I need to stay in touch with my sister. I can't tell you why."

Against his better judgment and without fully understanding why he should help her, Jack pulled open his desk drawn. He then easily pulled the cell from her fingers.

Haley looked wild eyed at him for a moment as he passed her back the phone.

"You're in luck," he said. "I have a Kodiak charger. It's old but it should work. Here."

Clutching both to her chest, she ran from the room and slammed the door.

"If you use that phone to call Ricky Rojas," Jack shouted after her. "I'll kill you myself."

She was shaking and horrified to learn that because of Jenna's foolish involvement with Ricky, two good men were dead. Was she less guilty?

Fear and anxiety knotted inside her and she gasped in terror. Hiding her head in the pillows, she sobbed desperately wishing she could turn back the clock to the moment when Frank and the other men had barged into the hotel room. She should have told them the truth then but she hadn't.

But what if she had? A small voice argued. Would the men be any less dead if Jenna had been in the safe house instead of her? All four could be dead, Jenna could be dead.

There was no absolution for her and she would have to accept her part in this but now she held the charger in her hand. Finding a socket behind the nightstand, she plugged it in. The little phone brightened with color and the little screen said charging. Hot tears streamed down her cheeks as she tried to hold her emotions in check. Consumed by her sins and brought on by her need to protect her sister, her body continued to shake as waves of weariness and despair swept over her. Unable to let go of the hollow feeling inside her, she slowly drifted into a troubled sleep.

A soft rapping at the door some forty-five minutes later woke her. She immediately turned to find the cell phone fully charged. It was Jack.

"Jenna," he said his voice was hard and demanding. "We need to talk."

"All right," Haley called out to him, fearing somehow he had learned the truth or worse, Jenna had been found dead. She wiped her tear stained face and joined him in the living room. Nervous, she sat on the couch and waited for him to speak.

Jack sat across from her, bold and intimidating. A lethal calmness made his dark eyes almost black.

"Frank called while you were sleeping, and he told why you are running from your boyfriend."

A cold knot formed in her stomach. She looked down at the floor, not wanting him to see the relief in her eyes. He didn't know about Jenna. She must be still alive. Still, she needed to know why Jenna was on the run. Her heart was pounding wildly as the looked up at his handsome face. She waited breathless moments for him to continue.

"You're little secret is out, Jenna," he snapped. "No wonder there is a price on your head."

"I don't know what you are talking about," Haley stammered trying to keep emotion out of her eyes.

"Do you have a death wish?" Jack asked angrily. "Did you think you could get away with something like this?"

Haley shifted in her seat.

"What are you talking about?" She said in a broken whisper.

"I'm talking about the eight million dollars you stole from Ricky Rojas."

CHAPTER FIVE

Haley's knees threatened to crumble under her and she collapsed back to the sofa.

Oh my god, Jenna, her soul screamed in silence, you stole eight million dollars from the Rojas Drug Cartel? Her heart was pounding in her chest. Her breath was raw and a sickening wave of terror was welling up in her belly.

"Frank is being pressured to get you back to the U.S. Marshals. They're making arrangements for you to get back to them now."

"Then take me back to Miami," she said, her body weighted with heaviness. "I don't want anyone else hurt because of me."

Jack sat across from her. He was unprepared for her tears. "Look, this isn't any of my business."

"No," Haley sniffed, "if anyone deserves an apology, it's you. Jack, I can't tell you what's going on because I don't know and I don't have eight million dollars."

Her eyes grew large and liquid. He should be furious but she was hard to hate and her tears were melting away his anger. It took what strength he had not to pull her protectively into his arms. He knew he had been taken by a vortex of lies and at the moment he didn't care.

Running his fingers through his hair, he studied her sad expression. What if she was telling the truth? Eight million dollars was a lot of money to hide.

He softened his voice and asked, "Does this have something to do with the phone call you are expecting?"

Haley nodded. "Yes. It has everything to do with this call. I'm sorry that you've been placed in this position. Just get me to a hotel room and leave me there. No one will know but you. You can call Frank. I'll be safe with the Marshals."

"Like you were last time?" Jack snapped. "And, I am not going to dump you off at some motel and come slinking back here, so get that out of your mind."

Haley shook her head. He had to listen. "Jack please, you've done enough. You don't need to get involved any deeper. I can't and won't ask you to do more. If you give me about ten minutes I'll get my things together. I'll be safe enough."

A sense of urgency drove him across the room. He pulled her into his arms. His fingers dug gently into her arms.

"No," he said with the warmth of his breath upon her. "You are staying with me."

His mouth was dangerously close to hers and they both knew it. His powerful gaze studied her face. His lips were almost upon hers as he said slowly, "Look, I, that is, you're not going anywhere."

Her cheeks colored under the heat of his gaze. The smoldering flame in his eyes startled her. She moved slightly forward, driven by her own passion. Explosive current raced through her and her fingers ached to reach out and touch him. She was electrified by his touch, his eyes and longed for the protectiveness of him arms and for the sweetness of his kiss. A hot ache grew in her throat. His lips were too close.

Jack felt the blood surge from his fingertips and spread with lightening speed through his body. He shouldn't have touched her. He shouldn't have brought her into his arms. Shock ran through his system and he realized he was dangerously close to kissing her lips. She was intoxicating and her closeness was like a drug, lulling him into insanity. Jack knew if he held her one more minute, he would kiss her and if he did, he didn't want to stop. Gently pushing her away took the last of his strength. "Look, let's cook some burgers."

"I'm not hungry," Haley protested.

"I am," Jack said in a husky whisper. He let his hand slide down her silky arm to her fingers. Using what self restraint he had left, he drew her into the kitchen.

Like a child in wonder, Haley helplessly followed. What had just happened? She asked herself. Her heart was thundering.

In the kitchen, Jack brought out a package of ground beef from the refrigerator. She remembered seeing some lettuce in the cooler. She would make a salad and try to grasp a world that was spinning out of control. Glancing at him, she realized he had for whatever reason positioned himself between her and danger. She only knew she wanted him there.

Across from her, Jack flipped on the large commercial fryer and brought out a bag of frozen French fries. Waiting for the oil to get hot, he formed the hamburger into patties before tossing them onto the grill.

Each occupied with the mindless activity of fixing dinner, they said nothing to one another.

Jack looked at Haley. She was still an enigma to him. She had seemed genuinely surprised he called her on the eight million dollars. Was it because he had found out her secret or was there something more? She evoked conflicting emotions in him and he was torn between wanting to protect her and the logical conclusion that she could not be trusted until she trusted him with her secret.

He knew little of Ricky Rojas but he knew of the Rojas Cartel. They were not to be trifled with and yet this little wisp of pure femininity had not only gotten away from Ricky but had taken eight million dollars of his money. The only thing that stood between her and Ricky was him. With a wry smile, he raised an eyebrow and winked at her. That was going to be Ricky's bad luck.

"It's so quiet here," Haley said breaking the silence between them.

Jack flipped the burgers; they were almost done. Dropping the fries into the oil, he said, "For the first two years, I thought I had traveled to the end of the world. The last two I know I have."

Despite herself Haley laughed. She looked at Jack realizing how much and how little she knew of this man and now, even now knowing the circumstances he was willing to risk his life for her. Why? She had been dumped unceremoniously on his lap and he had fed her, clothed her and for the most part was on relatively good behavior. She deserved less.

His eyes seemed ever upon her, watching her. What was he thinking? She wasn't Jenna; did he know? Did he guess?

Her thoughts drifted to Ricky Rojas. She had met Ricky only once, at lunch with Jenna and him aboard his yacht. Haley had thought Ricky handsome with strong Castilian features, amazingly warm eyes, black hair and old world manners that had impressed her at the time. No one had bothered to introduce her to the two large Hispanic men who stood arms folded hovering at the back of the boat.

"His bodyguards," Jenna had whispered.

While she had never met anyone with bodyguards, she dismissed the two men and concentrated on Jenna and her latest flame. Ricky was simply rich and that accounted for the men. Ricky and Jenna were unmistakably in love and for that Haley was glad.

Haley frowned as she sliced up the tomatoes. Surely, she

thought, Jenna must have known Ricky was involved in drugs. And now to learn Jenna had stolen eight million dollars of drug money? Haley shook her head. Jenna was many things but she wasn't a thief. There had to be more than this. There had to be!

She thought back over every conversation she had had with Jenna over the last year. She wished she had asked Jenna more questions about her life and Ricky. She wished Jenna had given her some clue as to where she had gone.

"Penny for your thoughts?" Jack asked with a grin and then laughed. "Never mind, I just remembered the eight million you have in your piggy bank."

Haley shook her head and gave him a playful frown. "I don't have eight million dollars Jack. I don't care who told you what, I don't have eight million dollars."

The look on her face told him she was telling the truth.

"The Feds think you have the money. Where would they get an idea like that?"

Haley shrugged. "I don't know."

"But you know who has the money, don't you?" He said with quiet emphasis. "What are you frightened of? Does this have something to do with the call you are waiting for?"

She didn't answer.

He reached in the cooler and grabbed two cold beers, offering her one. He would ask her again later.

The hamburgers were done and he placed two on his plate, one on hers and loaded both with golden French fries.

"Let's eat in the living room; mosquitoes will be out in force tonight."

Haley added tomato and lettuce to her hamburger and joined him on the couch.

Jack flipped on the TV news while they ate the burgers

and fries. No mention of an attack on the safe house, no mention that two U.S. Marshals were dead.

When they were finished, Haley took the dishes to the kitchen and returned with another beer for Jack and a diet coke for herself.

Jack was absorbed in a Robert De Niro movie. She sat next to him and tried to concentrate on the film.

Outside a fiery sunset gave way to the dusky hues of early nightfall before at last surrendering to an endless black sky filled with flickering stars.

Jack chuckled when he noticed she had fallen asleep beside him. His fingers slid sensually over her bare arm and he tried not to let the dark tendrils of hair curling lying across her dusky rose cheeks distract him.

He liked the way she felt beside him, curled up, trusting and warm. Her restful pose gave him an unobstructed view of her lovely cleavage and he tried to look away but the allure of her waist, the soft curve of her hips and nice round little bottom was giving the movie too much competition. He smiled, sure De Niro would understand.

She felt good beside him, too good and he saw no harm in finishing the movie with her lying next to him. Hell, it would be over in forty-five minutes. He reached over and turned off the lamp beside him. With his eyes heavy, the soft feel of a woman beside him, he felt himself drift off to a deep sleep.

He woke hours later to the cold tip of a gun pressed against his cheek. This time, he wasn't dreaming.

"You are in so much trouble, my friend," a dark-skinned Hispanic male hissed at him. "Ricky don't like anyone to touch his woman."

Jack was instantly awake. A sharp thrust of the shaft into the soft tissue of his neck. He saw the silhouette of a second man standing in front of him, blocking an infomercial. The blue light of the television cast a bizarre light about them.

Haley woke and pushed herself up to a sitting position. She screamed when she saw the men. She instinctively moved closer to Jack for protection. He kept his arm about her.

"Good evening, Ms. Jenna," the larger of the two said in a thick Spanish accent. "What? Do you forget your old friends Carlos and Diego? Did you think Ricky couldn't find you?"

Haley stared at the men. She recognized them from Ricky's yacht

Confident he had Jack's attention, the Columbian pulled away from Jack allowing him to take his first breath of air.

"So, who are you, Mister? DEA, FBI? CIA?" He demanded. He gave his companion a sneer and said, "Diego, he cannot be a Marshall, we shot all of them last night."

"Go to hell" Jack snapped. His arm brought Haley closer but held his gaze on his gunmen.

"I know what you are Mister," Carlos said pointing the semiautomatic at Jack's head. "You are a dead man."

"No, please!" Haley cried finding her voice. "I will go with you but you must leave him alone."

"Who is he?" Carlos demanded.

"Nobody," Haley cried rising to her feet. "He's nobody at all. He knows nothing. Just a friend I came to."

Carlos looked at Haley. "Jenna, your man is concerned about you .He wants you to come home."

"I'll go with you; leave this man alone." Haley said angrily. Realizing they thought she was her twin, Haley knew she had only one chance if she and Jack would survive the next few minutes. She had to become Jenna. Jenna would expect and demand the men to follow her orders. I can do this, she told herself walking directly to Carlos. Her mouth tightened with displeasure. "If for one minute you think Ricky will be pleased to know you manhandled me or my friend, you'd best think again. Now, let me get a few things and I will be with you."

"If you run again," Diego drawled in a thick Hispanic accent, "I will kill your friend."

"I won't run," Haley replied in a cool voice and walked with stiff dignity to the bedroom. Fearing she would collapse before she reached the door, she grabbed the doorknob and slipped into the room.

Out of their sight, she gasped for air. Adrenaline pushing her forward, she grabbed her bag of clothes and slipped into her shoes. With a cold fist closing over her heart, she padded her left pocket, the cell was there.

Grabbing the Kodiak charger, she said a prayer. There was no escape for her without putting Jenna or Jack in danger. Summing up what courage she could find, she swallowed hard. She had fooled the Federal Marshals, the FBI and even Jack, but none had known Jenna. Diego and Carlos were for the moment duped but Ricky would know. Jenna would be in mortal danger. Her breath was caught in her throat and she felt her heart pounding inside her chest.

"Okay," she said returning to Jack's living room. "Let's get out of here."

Walking across the room, she barely glanced at either of the men and she knew if she saw contempt in Jack's eyes, her legs would have failed her.

"Get up!" Diego snapped at Jack.

Jack stood rising above the Columbian.

"He isn't involved," Haley snapped. She barely recognized her angry command; it wasn't hers, but Jenna's. Fear for Jack made her bold. She positioned herself between Jack and Carlos.

"You will leave this man." she hissed. "I agreed to come with you. Now do as I say, leave him."

"It's okay," Jack interjected. "I don't think they were going to leave me here alive anyway."

Carlos leaned into Haley and hissed, "Who is this man to you, Jenna? A lover?"

Haley forced herself to remain rigid and met Carlos's mocking gaze with rage.

"Carlos, we'll take him to Ricky," Diego intervened. "Let Rojas put a bullet in his head. It will make an easier trip and we don't have to travel far."

Haley stiffened and dropped her head slightly. She held her gaze steady in cool warning. She would let no harm come to this man. She held her ground one more breathless minute.

Carlos dropped his gaze and lowered the semiautomatic.

She had won precious moments.

"Stop this foolishness. Get them out to the car," Diego ordered. Carlos waved his gun toward the door and Diego began grabbing a stack of newspapers and laid them by the curtains. Pulling a small cigarette lighter from his pocket, he lit the pile. The paper exploded into an orange-red glow as the paper melted into the flame.

"What are you doing?" Haley screamed, "No! Stop!"

Diego watched the fire grow in a low guttural voice he said, "Jenna, you should have thought of that before you came here."

"Do as he says," Jack warned her as he allowed himself to be pushed into the kitchen door. Haley caught the hard look in Jack's eyes and knew he wasn't going down without a fight.

With flames racing up the curtains, fire was instantly licking the ceiling. It was already too late to save the house.

Diego moved to the back bookcase and began pulling books into a second pile.

"Come on, Jenna," Carlos said with a wicked laugh, "Ricky is waiting."

Knowing the man would be the greater danger; Carlos moved behind Jack and pushed him through the front restaurant.

Lagging slightly, Haley looked around for something, anything. Then she saw it, the whiskey bottle Jack had left on the table from the night before.

Jack and Carlos walked through the restaurant, and she wasn't sure if either of them had realized she had fallen behind.

Hearing Diego behind her, she grabbed the bottle of Jack Daniels by the neck. Diego was on her heels. The moment he cleared the door, she swung with full strength hitting him squarely in the face.

Diego fell in a lump to the floor. He was out cold.

Haley ran through the restaurant and out the front door.

"Carlos, come quick," she screamed, hiding the whiskey bottle behind her back.

Carlos looked at Jack, "You move. You die."

He hurried up the porch and past Haley just as she swung the bottle hitting him in the back of the head. Carlos fell forward. Twisting, he turned on Jenna who stood with the bottle in her hand prepared to swing again.

"Save Diego," she hissed, "before he burns alive."

At the other side of the house, the fire was crackling and its breathe was a rasping howl. Carlos struggled to his feet. Cursing her in Spanish, he hurried back into the restaurant.

Damn her, Jack thought with a laugh.

Dropping the bottle, Haley ran to him.

"Let's get the hell out of here," Jack said pulling her to him. "My keys are in the house. This car is locked."

"Can we make it to Flamingo?" Haley cried looking in the direction of the marina.

"NO!" Jack screamed grabbing her hand. "Follow me!"

He pulled her hard toward the boat rentals. Passing the canoes and kayaks, he jumped into one of the two airboats resting on the bank. Two snaps on the center console, and the airboat roared to life sending a blast of wind behind them.

Haley climbed into the passenger seat of the two seated airboat. No seatbelts, she grabbed to the small metal hand rail beside her.

With his left hand on the steering shaft, and his right on the throttle, Jack brought the airboat just in time for Haley to see Carlos drag Diego from the house.

Rich red and orange flames were already climbing into the night sky.

"Your home!" Haley screamed over the roar of the flames. "Jack, I'm so sorry."

Even in the darkness, Haley watched Jack's eye twist into a wry smile.

"Don't be!" Jack spat watching his home burn up into flames, "I've wanted to burn the place down myself for years."

Jack turned the airboat hard into the Everglades.

"Hurry!" Haley cried but Jack was busy sending the airboat into the darkness.

CHAPTER SIX

Orange and red fiery fingers shot into the black night sky. The dark waters of the canal shivered with the burning images and silver and black smoke billowed from windows and doors of Jack's Bait Shop and his home.

Haley's fingers locked on the small hand rail as an explosive blast of air from the airboat's powerful engine forced the trim eight foot frame to glide across the narrow canal.

Turning from the waterway, Jack veered the airboat toward a low bank.

Haley braced herself as the airboat shot atop long strands of sawgrass like a pelican skimming the waters of Florida Bay.

With wind whipping her hair, arms and face, the river of grass parted as Jack drove the boat at breakneck speed through wall after wall of grass, sliding over gator holes and around cypress trees.

With speeds exceeding 48 mph, they covered their first quarter mile in 22 seconds. Quickly they traveled a full two miles from Pirates Cove in under than two minutes.

In heavy darkness, Jack dropped the plane. With no water to carry it, the airboat almost stalled in the water. Jack spun the watercraft around in a razor-sharp turn toward his house and bait shop. The boat came to a leisurely stop atop the grassy wet bottom of sawgrass. A back wash of water eased into the boat, far below their feet, before rolling off into the bog.

Haley's pulse had yet to slow. Small hairs on her arm

quivered from the force of wind. Trembling, she kept her fingers tight around the hand rail.

From their distance, they both sat silent watching the house fire burn high into the night sky. Against the flames that shot skyward, they watched the dark silhouette of a sedan move away from the inferno. The high beams cut into the night as it was driven across the small bridge and recklessly away from the blaze.

"They aren't going to give up until they find you," Jack said, his face hardening into a dark mask. Miniature flames from the fire were reflecting in his cold eyes. His voice was soothing yet cool with contempt and his warning clear.

A terrifying realization washed over her. She knew he would be ready for them the next time. With her senses drugged and her breath shallow, she said softly, "You saved my life."

A sensuous light from the fire burned between them. He chuckled. His eyes changed from hard ice to warm velvet brown. He made no attempt to conceal the sexual magnetism he wore like a second skin.

Taking in her small frame, his lips parted into a seductive grin. "No, you saved us. You and that bottle."

Haley bit her lip to hide a nervous smile. She had only reacted to fear. Fear for Jenna and fear for Jack and herself.

"I was too scared to think," she stammered under her breath.

"Don't kid yourself, Jenna," Jack said, his husky voice sending a pink blush to her cheeks. "You saved both our lives. What happened to Diego?"

Haley swallowed hard.

"I hit him in the head," Haley said softly, "he went out cold."

Jack laughed out loud; the sound of it captivated her. His gaze riveted on her face, then moved slowly over her body. "Good, he deserved it. Do you still have your cell phone?"

"Yes. Why?"

"We're going to need it but first things first. I have a buddy who lives a short way from here, Billy Two Bears. He'll help us out. We've got to get out of the 'glades."

A large bull alligator was staring up at Haley, resting in the water only four inches away from the airboat. His eyes blinked and he lowered his massive body into the dark waters as Jack snapped the switch and allowed the airboat to glide its way through the Everglades.

As the moon broke across on the eastern sky, Jack slowly pulled into a small encampment. They were too far away to make out the details but Haley could see a small cabin, a chicken coop and several animal pens covered with palm fronds.

A tall handsome Seminole silently approached the boat. His stride was smooth, his body alert to their arrival. Dark skinned with deep set ebony eyes and his long black hair gathered in a pony tail that fell down his back, he wore faded jeans and a red and white plaid shirt cut at the shoulders revealing muscular arms. Billy Two Bears, Haley concluded as she watched him approach. With the sure movements of a Florida panther, he moved smoothly through the tall grass toward the airboat.

"Saw the fire. Was that your place?" the Indian asked. A faint light twinkled in the depths of his black eyes and a half smiled touched his mouth.

"Yeah," Jack said with a backward glance from his shoulder. He climbed down from the airboat and offered Haley his hand.

The warmth of his touch was reassuring and intoxicating. As she rose to stand, he slipped his powerful hands about her small waist and lifted her from the airboat. Gently setting her beside him, Jack turned to the Seminole.

"Billy, I need to borrow your truck for a couple of days."

"Take it," Billy replied with an appreciative glance at Haley. Reaching in his back pocket, he threw the keys at Jack as easily as he could have thrown a bowie knife into the chest of an enemy.

With the fiery blaze in the distance, Jack grabbed the keys mid air and clutched them in his fist.

"What about your airboat?" Billy said as he helped Jack pull the airboat onto the grassy bank.

"Keep it, Billy," Jack said stepping away from it. "I'm not coming back. I'll leave your truck in town, okay?"

Billy looked at Haley; the double meaning of his gaze was obvious. Turning to Jack, he said, "Sure. No problem."

Jack reached out and offered his hand to Billy Two Bears. Billy took Jack's hand and held it for a moment. Friendship and respect was confirmed in their hard grasp. With a nod of his head, Jack turned and motioned for Haley to follow him to the truck.

"Where're we going?" Haley asked as they pulled away from the encampment.

"Away from here," Jack answered. He gave her body a raking glance. "We'll head into the Keys."

As they drove away, Haley twisted back in her seat and she saw Billy Two Bears, his arms crossed over his chest as he watched the truck drive away.

"He didn't ask any questions." Haley said turning back to Jack.

"In the 'glades, there's a code. Don't ask, don't tell. Billy's a friend, I'll miss him."

"What about your home?"

His jaw clenched and his eyes slightly narrowed. "I won't miss that."

"But you've just lost everything," Haley said. A tumble of confused thoughts and emotions tore at her. Her cross was heavier now. He had just given up everything for her. Before she could say more, Jack grinned. "We still have your eight million dollars."

Their eyes met. Shock ran through her. Her heart came to an abrupt stop and she choked back a protest.

Jack laughed.

"I don't want your money, Jenna," Jack said evenly but suddenly Haley wasn't sure.

Unwelcome tension tightened between them. What was the truth? Black fright swept through her. Fearful images were building in her mind. Could she trust Jack Morgan? She suddenly wasn't sure. She wasn't sure of anything.

Drawing a cool breath, she knew she needed him, she had no choice. Using anyone, no matter how despicable their motives, was not her style, but her sister's life was hanging in the balance. Ricky Rojas had sent men to kill her twice.

Haley had never truly given Jack her trust and what little she had given him was gone.

Jack focused on the drive. Sure of his route, he took the dirt road from Billy Two Bears far faster than was safe. What his pretty companion didn't know was they were probably still playing a deadly game of cat and mouse with the Columbians. Carlos and Diego were traveling a parallel highway to the road they were on. Jack hoped they had enough of a head start to hit the main highway ahead of them. Jack and Haley had a bit of a slight advantage but both roads crossed ahead. He hit the accelerator knowing they had to reach five points before they did.

A rich under growth crowded both sides of the single lane road. A thick mixture of royal palms and the tropical hardwoods of gumbo limbo, strangler figs and poison woods made the road dark and insolated them within a high wall of foliage. Gradually, heavy trees and heavy brush gave way to slow moving sawgrass and the road changed from dirt to asphalt.

Jack looked down the highway and saw no other vehicles. He turned toward Florida City and Homestead.

Beside him, his pretty companion had sat quiet. He sensed something was troubling her but shrugged it off. The Columbians were no doubt on her mind; he reached over and slipped his hand over hers.

"There's nothing to fear, Jenna," he said softly.

His hand came down on hers and the mere touch of his skin sent warming shivers through her. His voice was silken and wrapped her like a warm summer blanket and while she would have longed for this comfort, she clung to the fear that he was only helping her for the money. Eight million was a lot of money; could she blame him? Though his words were warm and reassuring, Haley couldn't trust her heart, not when her sister's life was depended on it.

"I want to borrow your cell phone," he said.

Obediently she handed it to him, sure that as long as he thought she had the money, he would no doubt placate her every whim.

With his left hand on the steering wheel, the cell firm in his right, he scarcely looked down as he punched a phone number with his thumb. Haley knew he would be calling Frank.

"Hey buddy!" he said in a voice that was deceptively calm.

Haley watched his eyes narrow though he took great care to keep his voice crisp and clear. He hit the speaker phone and put his index finger over his mouth as he laid the Kodiak on the dash.

"You're alive," Frank said sounding almost surprised. "A call just came in about your home. Is Jenna with you?"

"Yeah, she's with me." Jack answered him with a glance toward Haley. "I thought you were the only one who knew she was with me. What happened? Who did you talk to?"

"Only one, Jack," Frank answered him, his voice was heavy, "My supervisor, that's it, I swear. He must have told someone. I'll find out who. Look, where are you? I need to get both of you to a safe place."

Jack shook his head at Haley as he answered Frank. "I don't think that's a good idea. Everything is hot right now. Look, I'll call you in the morning. We're going to get some rest. We may need it."

"Okay, I'll arrange a pick up then."

Jack turned off the Kodiak. He handed it back to Haley.

"We're going back to the Marshals tomorrow?" she choked; her breath seemed to have solidified in her throat. Her relief was short lived as Jack spat, "Hell no!"

"But you said..." she protested.

Jack's fingers tightened on the steering wheel, the muscles of his forearm hardened. "What I said and what we're going to do are two different things."

"This is about the money, isn't it?" came Haley's quick retort. She regretted her words the minute they were spoken.

Jack glared at her. His eyes grew hard.

"No, this isn't about the money, Jenna. I don't like someone coming into my home holding a gun at my head and then burning everything I own to the ground. This may have started with you but I'm in the game now."

Haley had seen the icy contempt in his eyes and she looked away. She knew the hate was directed to Ricky Rojas. His expression darkened with an unreadable emotion. She prayed his male pride wasn't going to get them all killed.

"Look, we'll be in Florida City in minutes," Jack warned her, "keep you eyes open. Our friends may be close."

Haley nodded. Jack was right; they could trust no one. But could she trust him? No longer able to differentiate between what was real and what covered a lie, she stared out the window.

It was late and in the sleepy little town of Florida City, the only vehicle on the road was a police car. Jack waved the officer as they passed.

When they reached U.S 1, Jack turned right and began the long trek into the Keys.

Passing up several nice hotels in Key Largo, Tavernier, Plantation and Islamorada, Jack finally stopped in front of a small hotel in Matecumbe.

He sat behind the wheel just a moment stretching his long arms and legs.

"Wait here," he told Haley as he went to awaken the motel owner.

Haley watched him knock at the door and a moment later a light came on inside a tiny office as the sleepy motel owner came to let Jack in the room. She watched him sign in, pay cash for a room before returning to the truck.

Jack drove to four doors down and parked the truck in front of a motel room.

"Honey," he said with a grin. "We're home."

Gathering her bag of clothes, she followed Jack to the red door with the brass number four on the front. He slipped the key into the lock and turned the door handled.

The motel, the room was neat, clean and looked recently refurbished. Three brightly colored ocean prints hung on the wall but did little to brighten the room. A black phone, radio alarm clock and TV remote control lay atop the nightstand. A twenty-seven inch TV rested on one side of the dresser along with a welcome note and menus of nearby restaurants.

Jack snapped the room air conditioner on high and threw himself on the bed. He grabbed the remote control on and began flipping channels.

Haley stood stupidly at the door clutching her bag of clothes. Her eyes fixated on the double bed.

"It's all they had," Jack explained watching her. His eyes flashed in a familiar display of impatience. "Don't worry; I'm too damn tired to think of anything but sleep."

Haley took a breath and nodded.

"Go take a shower and look, if I come in, I'll knock," Jack promised looking already tempted to break his word.

Haley blushed and nodded hurrying toward the small bathroom.

Stripping off her clothes, she kept one eye toward the door and took a quick shower. Drying herself, she reached in the plastic bag of clothes and pulled out a T-shirt. It fell to her thighs. It would have to do.

When she returned to the room, Jack was asleep on the bed. She gently eased to the empty side of the bed and pushed back the covers. She quietly laid the cell phone on the nightstand and turned off the TV.

Slipping under the covers next to him, she was conscious of his hard lean body stretching across the double bed. His body heat warmed the sheets, and within her, she could hear her heart hammering in her ears. She tried to keep her breath steady but his nearness was overpowering. Gathering the covers around her, she turned her back to him. Was she safe with him? Did she want to be?

Her pulse swelled and it seemed her heart had risen from its usual place. The musky smell of him caused blood to surge from her fingertips to her toes. She lay still, she was exhausted. The hum of the air conditioner, the coolness of the room weighed heavily on her eyelids and despite the unfamiliar presence of his body that captured her every thought, she felt whatever his motive he would keep her safe.

With wisps of sleep dulling her senses, she slowly closed her eyes.

The cell phone rang, sending a high shrill through the darkness. Haley grabbed the cell; she had so carefully placed on the nightstand moments earlier.

"Jenna!" Haley cried into the cell.

In the darkness, she felt Jack twist. He was awake.

"Where are you?"

"I'm in Key West!" Jenna said breathlessly.

The light snapped on next to her. Jack rose in bed.

"Haley," Jenna pleaded, "I don't have time to talk. Ricky is after me!"

Haley relived the raid on the FBI Safe house and her miraculous escape through the Everglades.

"I know," was all Haley could say before Jenna asked, "Where are you?"

"I'm in Upper Matecumbe Key," Haley said trying not to look at Jack.

"What? I don't understand. I thought you'd be safe with the Marshals. How did you get into the Keys?"

"It's a long story," Haley said wearily. "What's going on?"

"Can you meet me in Key West tonight? I'll tell you everything."

"All right Jenna" she said firmly. "Just tell me one thing. Did you steal eight million dollars?

There was a pause.

"Yes," came Jenna's soft reply, "But it's not what you think. Haley, I need you to trust me. Look, I know it sounds strange to say this but I did what I did for both of us. I was afraid that Ricky or someone in his family might have come for you as well. I did what I did to keep us both safe, Haley. It was the only way out for both of us. Be ready to meet me around midnight. I'll see you then. I love you."

Haley wanted to say more but the line was dead.

She slowly turned to Jack noting his handsome face was set, his mouth clamped and his eyes fixed on her. He rose from the bed and walked to the TV before he turned back to her.

She swallowed hard.

"So, you're not Jenna Rollins" he said his voice edged with steel. Seeing his eyes flash in anger, Haley almost recoiled from his hard expression. Taking in every inch of her body, he asked in a cool voice, "Who the hell are you?"

Haley sat upright. She had to tell him the truth. "I'm Haley Rollins, Jenna's sister."

Jack stared at her. "How could you pass for her? I mean..."

"We're twins," Haley interrupted him, "identical twins."

Jack sat silent.

Looking up at his stilled expression, Haley said softly, "Jenna wants me to meet her in Key West tonight."

"What about the eight million dollars?"

"It's real."

Jack's dark brown eyes blazed with sudden anger. "Do you two play this sort of thing often? No wonder you have men shooting at you."

Haley gathered her legs protectively close to her chest. Biting her lip, she looked away. "Will you take me to Key West? If you won't I'll find a way there myself. I have to get to my sister."

Jack took a long breath. "What did you say your name was, Haley?"

"Yes, it's Haley. Until two days ago, I was a manager of a small bookstore in Vero Beach," Haley snapped meeting his gaze. "This hasn't been easy on me either."

Jack's laughter ripped through the air. He should have been angrier with her but relief washed over him. He'd been right about her all along. This was no party girl and she didn't belong to Ricky Rojas. Whatever harsh word he had meant to cut her with was lost in her soft blue eyes that were misty and frightful. She was telling the truth.

She sat upright, her small figure regal and curving, ready to accept whatever punishment he was ready to throw at her.

"My sister called me two days ago," she explained breathlessly, "She said she was in trouble. I drove to Miami and met her at a motel. Before she could tell me what was going on, the U.S. Marshals barged down the door. Jenna slipped out the bathroom window."

Jack took in the melting softness of her body. Her blue eyes held soft shadows. He longed to take away her fear. Instead, he answered in a cool tone, "And the Marshals believed you were your sister?"

"Yes, I told you, we are identical twins. I thought being her for a few days would keep her safe," Haley said in a whisper. Her long brown hair framed her heart shaped face. He heard the truth in her voice and saw the same strength she had used to cold cock the Columbians. It did not lessen her femininity or her vulnerably. Waiting for the fallout of her words, her lips were firm and sensual revealing a stubborn streak that he could only admire.

Straightening her shoulders, she said with a determined little glint to her chin, "I can see now, I was wrong."

Jack stared at Haley. God, she was so beautiful.

Haley held her profile strong and rigid. "Truth is, only our grandmother could ever tell the difference. When we were little, we even practiced writing like each other. I would take her place for tests at school. I understand how wrong I was for always giving her an easy way out but she's my sister."

"You take care of those you love." Jack said softly. "Jenna is lucky and I understand why you did what you did, Haley."

Moving closer to her, he sat down beside her and asked the one question that was burning him alive. "So did you leave a husband back in Vero Beach?"

She shook her head. "No. No husband, no boyfriend."

Jack felt drops of moisture on his damp forehead and raked his hand through his hair as he asked, "What about Haley? Who is she?"

"A little mouse whose is afraid of her own shadow," Haley sobbed unable to hold herself in check a moment longer. She could fight his anger but not his kindness.

Jack smiled. "Haley, you are no mouse. You have successfully evaded one of the biggest drug dealers in south

Florida. Twice! And hitting Diego and threatening Carlos took quite a bit of courage. By the way, have you even met those two men before or for that matter, Ricky Rojas? Did you know them?"

"Once, about eight months ago. I had lunch with Jenna and Ricky on his yacht. I remember Carlos and Diego were hanging around us. Jenna said they were Ricky's bodyguards."

"What is he like, this Angel De La Morte?"

Haley shuttered. "He's very charming. Good looking and seemed devoted to my sister. In fact other than a few polite words to me, his eyes were only for her."

"Would he know you weren't your sister if he saw you?"

Haley looked down at her hands and twisted them. "How could he not?"

Jack grunted. "What do you know about Jenna's life?"

"She moved to South Beach after high school and worked as a hostess at some trendy restaurant before being hired by one of the most prestigious modeling firms in Miami."

It was impossible to keep pride out of her voice. "She met Ricky at one her haunts in South Beach. They fell in deeply in love with each other."

Jack arched an eyebrow. "Then she stole eight million dollars from him."

Haley was quiet.

"What did she say to you on the phone?"

"She wants me to meet her in Key West tonight. She said she could explain everything then."

Jack said nothing. Long breathless minutes passed.

"Can you take me there?" Haley asked again.

"I'll take you there," Jack agreed. He watched as Haley's small shoulders fell; gratitude filled her eyes.

"Look, I guess we should try to get some sleep." He said evenly, "I think we are safe enough here tonight."

"What about the U.S. Marshals?" Haley asked, "Are you going to tell them about Jenna?"

Jack shook his head. "No, not right now. Right now, we need some shut eye. Tomorrow I'll get you to Key West."

Jack returned to the bed, and snapped the light off. Once again she felt the strength of his masculine body lying next to her.

Digesting all she had said to him, he stretched his long legs out. Part of him was already arguing the logic of his offer but he had eight million reasons to get her to Key West and he was falling for her lies and her soft wide eyed innocence. He was falling alright, he chided himself; hook, line and sinker. What the hell was he supposed to do, he argued back, leave her to fend for herself? And what about the Feds, he thought. What did he owe them? Nothing.

Rolling over to his side, he heard her soft breathing beside him. What the hell have you gotten yourself into, sport, he asked himself turning back to her. There was no where for his arms except around her.

In the darkness, he heard her soft voice. "Jack, why are you doing this for me?"

"Hell, I don't know," he said under his breath as not to disturb the darkness. "To help you. To help Frank. For revenge. I don't know for sure but I do know this: for the first time in a long time I feel alive."

"Thank you," she said in a soft voice sounding very tired.

It seems only minutes before he felt her body go limp as she drifted into a sound sleep.

Jack lay still. He was too damn tired to think about the Columbians and where they might be. He was too worn out to think about putting together a plan for a meeting tomorrow with her sister.

Her breath was warm and moist against his chest. It felt good to feel strong and protective again. It was good to know he was once again a hunter, not some damn rabbit hiding at the end of the world. Instinctively, he knew he would do what he had to tomorrow to save Haley and himself.

She shifted slightly and turned into him, pushing her full breasts against his chest. God, how he wanted to cup those beautiful breasts and bury his face in them. A smooth silky leg brushed against him and slid slowly up his thigh. His body responded in a shutter. She felt warm as she snuggled deeper into his arms; he felt her trust. He needed her trust; he needed another human being to trust him, need him.

"Haley," he said softly gathering her to him. He liked the sound of that name.

Holding her, he knew he would sleep peacefully in her arms this night. Tomorrow would come soon enough.

A small smile touched his lips; this wasn't the first time he had played high stakes poker. His gut was telling him he should fold and walk away but he was betting on the lady. And one more reason, he thought holding her close: eight million dollars was riding on how he played this hand.

CHAPTER SEVEN

Haley woke to the slam of a metal door. She bolted upright to find Jack standing by the door. He grinned. "Sorry, I was trying to be quiet."

Haley slowly fluttered her long lashes and the corners of her mouth curved seductively into a smile that took his breath away. Jack stood stupidly at the door watching her.

Seeing the soft swell of her full breasts beneath her t-shirt, a wave of desire passed over him. He shifted from one leg to the other like a nervous teen. She is exquisite, he thought taking in her gentle and overwhelming beauty. How could she be so soft, alluring and powerfully sexy, and not even know it.

Tiny curls escaped a heavy silken mass of thick dark hair and perfectly framed her delicately oval face. His gaze naturally fell to the silky satin of an exposed thigh.

At the moment all he could think of was pulling her hot little body into his arms. What it would be like to be loved by such a woman, he wondered, then remembered he was only along for the ride. Besides, he had eight million reasons to keep her near. At the moment he didn't give a damn about one of them. He knew she would lay down her life for her sister and for him. He doubted either one of them deserved her loyalty.

Haley felt a warm glow flow through her at the sight of him. With no idea of the reaction she would cause, she stretched her arms over her pushing her taunt little nipples into the t-shirt.

"I didn't mean to sleep so long," she said lazily settling back against the headboard.

"There's a fast food joint across the street. I went over to get coffee," Jack explained taking the small tray to her bedside. He dumped half bag of condiments on the nightstand next to her cup. "I didn't know how you liked it, so I grabbed everything."

Haley giggled softly surveying a half bag of sugar, blue and pink packets of sweetener and cream. He must have cleaned out the restaurant's condiment trays.

Adding a single packet of sweetener to her coffee, she couldn't help but appreciate his well muscled body. His steady gaze was exciting and gave her a sense of protection. She could trust him, couldn't she?

Tonight, they would meet Jenna in Key West. She blushed realizing how selfish she was to want a bit more time with this dark handsome stranger. She took a sip of hot coffee and returned the Styrofoam cup to her nightstand. "You haven't changed your mind have you? I mean, you're going to…"

"To take you to your sister," Jack finished for her. "Yes, but first we're going to get something decent to eat. I'm not into fast foods and the continental breakfast offered by the motel is two-day-old donuts."

"When you finish your coffee," he said walking over to a chair by the motel window, "we'll go out, get some breakfast and head down to Key West. That's what you want, isn't it? To find your sister?"

Eager to close the distance between Matecumbe and Key West, Haley nodded. "It will take me just a minute in the bathroom. I'll hurry." With that, she hurried into the bathroom to wash her face.

Using a fluffy white cotton wash clothe to wipe her face, she studied her reflection in the mirror; her mind never far from Jack Morgan.

He was too good to be true and she once again wondered, why he was helping her? Should it matter? Yes, came the hot reply and she couldn't afford to be distracted by his ruggedly handsome face, his compelling brown eyes or the confident set of his shoulders. She couldn't afford to let her guard down because Jenna's life was held in his truth or in his lies. Was his interest humanitarian or was it something more?

And yet, she thought brushing her long brown hair, how much did she know of him? Was he really the General Manger of a Resort Casino or was he a murderer who turned in his friends to the FBI? All she truly knew was that he was in the witness protection program but he could be anyone. So could she. Today he would take her to Key West. She would know his real nature by day's end. She dressed quickly and tried to push apprehension and fear aside.

Wishing for something a bit more suitable than the plastic bag that held her clothes and makeup, she quickly applied mascara and added a touch of lip gloss to her lips..

Returning to him, she found him staring out the window and instantly regretted her doubts about him.

Seeing her, he smiled. "I think if we should keep moving in Billy's truck. No one will notice us in that banged up Chevy."

His eyes swept over her approvingly and he gave her a conspiratorial wink.

Haley offered him a soft smile; she would have crawled to Key West if she had to. Taking her last sip of her coffee, she said, "Any time you are ready."

She frowned as she placed the cup on the nightstand; realizing they had little to no money. "We're going to need cash today. I can take $ 300 out of an ATM for cash and use my credit cards for whatever else we need."

"No," came Jack's swift reply but he realized they had no choice. The Feds were probably watching his bank account.

"It's okay," she assured him. "This won't break me and we can't risk having anyone follow us by using your check card."

Jack gave her a grudging nod. "You have a cool head, Haley Rollins. I don't like taking money from a woman but, for now, you're right."

He studied her open, intelligent gaze, struck again that this was no ordinary woman.

"I'll pay you back," he said, his voice reeking with male pride. "For now, let's hit the road."

Haley followed him out of the room knowing in truth the money they needed would be used wholly on her behalf. Jack owed her nothing yet in his mind his old-fashioned chivalry demanded he pay their way. His honor and battered pride demanded he pick up the tab even though by right he had no responsibility to it. She'd worry about repaying him later.

Climbing into Billy Two Bears's truck, a sensuous light passed between them. They were touching more than the other's heart.

Jack drove less than a mile before they came upon a liquor store boasting an ATM. Without a word, Haley took cash from the ATM and passed it to Jack.

Tucking his money into his shirt pocket, he started up the truck and merged back into the light flow of traffic heading south.

Billy Two Bears's battered old brown truck ran smoothly, though without air conditioning, through Indian Key, to Duck and Conch Key before stopping at a small restaurant in Marathon.

The restaurant was small and filled with locals and a few tourists sharing tourist maps and brochures. No one noticed the two who went to a small table.

"Are you still serving breakfast?" Jack asked the waitress.

"Anything you want," she replied with a provocative glance at Jack. In her mid-thirties, the pretty redhead wore bright green Parrot Head shirt and white short shorts. She smiled at Jack and added, "Best buy is the Conch Special, two eggs, home fries, bacon, toast and your choice of orange or apple juice."

"Sounds good," Jack said with his eyes on Haley. "How 'bout you, princess?"

Haley blushed. "The same."

For a moment they sat like strangers idly looking around the crowded restaurant.

"If we don't talk to each another," Jack said with a grin, "people will think we're married."

Haley laughed. "That's true. Tell me more about you."

Jack frowned, his eyes grew dark and shadows crossed his face.

"Okay," Haley said quickly changing the subject, "If you could start over, right here, right now what would you do? Where would you go?"

Jack relaxed and an easy smile touched his lips.

"I know this one," he said in the words of a man with certainty. "If I were to start over, I'd go to some place as far from Las Vegas and the Everglades as I could find. I'd go to Europe, Greece, to be exact. A friend of mine there has a string of small but elegant hotels. I have a standing job offer. I would take him up on it. Have you ever been to Greece, Haley?"

Haley shook her head. "No, but I've heard it's beautiful. Then what?"

Jack's eyes danced with fire. "I'd find the right girl."

"And have a lot of Greek children?"

Jack laughed but his eyes held their gaze steady on her. "Yes, I'd have lots of children. Do you like children?"

The waitress returned with their coffee and juice,

"Yes," she said in a wistful reply, "I like children very much."

"Your turn," Jack said reaching over for a tiny container of cream. "What would you do?"

"Me? I don't know, I suppose that depends on Jenna. I have no idea how she's going to get out of this one but she always does. She's like a cat. No matter how high she falls, she always lands on her feet."

"Good to know," Jack said keeping his gaze steady, "but I asked about you."

Haley felt her face burn and once again felt lacking when compared to her adventurous sister. "I don't take chances."

"Do you want to play it safe?" He said in a husky open invitation.

Now she knew she was disappointing him. "Boring, huh? But I play it safe and I play it straight. I've never wanted what Jenna wanted: fame, fortune, glamour."

As their breakfast arrived, Jack moved away their coffee cups to the center of the table to make room for their breakfast platters.

"You told me what Jenna wants," he said slicing a large portion of ham, "I still haven't heard your answer."

Haley looked down at her food and decided to trust him with just one small dream. "I'd like to write travel articles," she began, "but my home, my family would always be first with me."

Jack said nothing.

"I've disappointed you," Haley said trying to hide in a laugh. "I'm afraid there's little call for old-fashioned girls these days."

Jack smiled. His eyes were gentle and contemplative. "Actually, I find it refreshing."

Haley took a long breath and several bites of scrambled egg. If her mouth was full, it would be impolite to talk. She didn't want to talk. She didn't want to share with him her secret desires. Why? She asked herself. Because her simple wishes sounded so much like his.

Breakfast it turned out was delicious and prepared to perfection. They finished their meal in silence, each absorbed in their own private thoughts. They gassed up before they left Marathon. Their next major destination was Seven Mile Bridge.

Traffic was light as they began their trek across what was once the longest bridge in the world. The sky above was baby blue and the waters surrounding them were a deep sea turquoise that spread for miles into the open seas.

Overhead seagulls rested on abandoned pilings and osprey competed with the fishermen.

Across from the bridge, a large schooner glided atop the shiny blue waters. From her vantage, Haley could make out the varnished mahogany with thick masks and halyards. The beautiful sleek 130 foot schooner glided across the waters. Her kind once filled the shipping lanes of the Caribbean avoiding the marauding pirates and buccaneers.

With the fresh scent of the ocean reviving her spirits, she felt renewed hope. Each passing mile brought them closer to her twin.

In no hurry to cross the big bridge, Jack had slowed Billy's old truck to enjoy the breathtaking view of sea and sky, but he pressed his foot against the gas pedal as soon as they reached Bahia Honda State Park.

Stopping for a quick break in Little Torch Key, they pushed on through the Lower Keys of Big Pine, Cudjoe, and Boca Chica Key before reaching tiny Stock Island and Key West.

It was middle of the afternoon and they were on the last mile of U.S. 1. Like any other sightseers, Jack drove down Palm Avenue to Duvall Street then on to South Street and Flagler Avenue.

The streets were busy with vacationers eager to make the most of their visit to Key West. They were easily separated from the locals who knew better than to rush to any destination.

Jack took a sharp turn off Fleming and stopped in front of a small single story home. Its signage read Aunt Molly's Bed and Breakfast.

The converted white wood frame home was nestled between a small restaurant and a two story Victorian home. Several thick green Boston ferns hung across the front porch and oversized white rockers gave visitors a comfortable view of the quaint neighborhood. It was within walking distance of Mallory Square but then every place on the island was in walking distance of everywhere else.

"This looks as good as any," Jack said squeezing the truck into a tight parking space. "And, I'd just as soon as avoid the larger hotels."

Eager to stretch her legs, Haley agreed.

They were halfway up the flowered walk when a plump matronly woman stepped out on the porch. Her blue eyes were bright and the wrinkles about her eyes and brow spoke of many good years.

"Any rooms available?" Jack called out to her.

Holding open the screen door, she motioned them up the walk. "Yes, child, come on in. I'm happy to have you."

Jack and Haley followed her inside the home, which was as neat and clean as its exterior.

In the foyer, a small desk served as guest check in and out. White ceiling fans whirled circulating the air and adding to the charming Key West décor and furnishings.

Behind it was a stunning sunset picture of Mallory Square. The colors were vibrant and the work excellent. Haley knew Key West had the benefit of a colony of artists, writers and poets. The picture, on consignment, had a small price tag in its bottom right corner and was for sale by one of them.

Noticing her interest, the woman smiled at Haley. "My favorite painting," their hostess said in a soft southern drawl, "but it's for sale if you like it. Is this is your first time here in Key West?"

She didn't give Jack or Haley a chance to answer. "Well, if this is your first time here, you'll want to take in the sunset at Mallory Square. It's where everyone gathers each evening to celebrate our favorite time of day."

Jack took the registration card she offered and began filling it in.

Looking down at the registration card, Haley felt her cheeks burn with color as she watched Jack sign them in as Mr. and Mrs. Smith. Oh please, she thought as blood pounded through her and her face grew hot with humiliation.

"I'm Aunt Molly," their hostess said cheerfully. "We have a nice little restaurant next door. Coupons are in your room. I serve Breakfast here every morning from six am until eleven. Coffee will be ready in the parlor a bit earlier. Breakfast isn't fancy but there is always plenty of it."

"Sounds great," Jack said giving Aunt Molly a dazzling smile. Aunt Molly's face was brightened by Jack's attention.

Handing Jack a room key, she said, "You two have yourselves a nice stay."

If Aunt Molly were interested in their shenanigans, she didn't give a clue. Haley smiled. Jack turned to her and smiled. "This looks comfortable."

"Yes," Haley agreed noting that for the second time in two days she would be sharing her bed with Jack Morgan.

CHAPTER EIGHT

I've been driving all day. Let's get out, go for a walk maybe pick up a few clothes."

Aunt Molly had discreetly vanished into the interior of the residence when Jack and Haley left the bed and breakfast. On Fleming, Haley was content to follow Jack's lead.

Colorful shops and boutiques filled every nook and small alleyway. Jack paused in front of one shop boasting handmade Cuban cigars but Haley playfully pushed him away informing him she hated the vile stench and couldn't have one around her without the smell giving her a headache.

For the most part, Haley guessed they appeared as other vacationing tourists as they skirted about street vendors offering tourists everything from corn fritters to silly hats and fedoras.

The motorized trolley passed them twice. On one pass, Haley caught part of the Tour Guide's narrative on the island's famous resident Ernest Hemingway.

She knew they were killing time but she took comfort in the bright afternoon wishing she had more time to explore the shops with their window displays of souvenirs, rum cake and island jewelry.

Jack stopped before Pirates Museum and Gift Shop. "Do we have time for a little sight seeing?"

"Yes," Haley cried in pleasure. "I'd love to see the museum."

They spent the next forty-five minutes touring the

museum's remarkable display of treasures, pirate history, and muskets and swords. Spanish doubloons, dazzling emeralds, copper relics, and Aztec artifacts were prominently displayed in lighted glass cases.

For Haley, each was more beautiful than the one before but it was the story of each piece that intrigued her, not the value assessed the items.

Jack surveyed her every move, watching her lovely blue eyes grow large and liquid as she read the information on each item. With a dreamy expression, she looked up at him once and tore his heart from his chest.

As a whole, he hadn't wanted much in his life and had settled in recent years for little, but with each passing moment, he knew he wanted her more than the air he breathed.

As most attractions do, the museum emptied out to a very busy gift shop where Haley continued her exploration of silver and gold coins. Jack watched her knowing she was content merely to look.

Resisting the warnings inside him, he pulled a clerk aside and quietly motioned to a Reale gold doubloon that hung on a diamond rope cut chain. Instinctively he knew the golden bezel skull and cross bone would please her. After all, it was late in the day; financial transactions would be posted the next. Tomorrow, they would be gone from Key West but tonight, she would wear a pirate's gold chain on her pretty neck and he would have the pleasure of knowing he had placed it there.

She was listening to a salesman explain about the delicacy of the craftsmanship to an overweight couple from New England when he came up behind her. Pulling her away from the counter, he gently slipped the necklace over her head and with pleasure watched it fall to her beautiful breasts.

A small gasp escaped her full lips and he brought his mouth down upon hers drinking in her sweetness.

Her lips were soft, moist and easily parted for him. Though it lasted only a moment she quivered at the tenderness of his kiss.

When he pulled away from her, his eyes were veiled with dark desire.

Haley reached up and caressed the coin. Caught off guard by the touch of his lips, she took a quick breath trying to slow the spirals of ecstasy that raced through her.

"Do you like it?" He asked, his voice a caress across her cheeks.

"Jack," she stammered, "you shouldn't have, I mean, I thought we agreed."

But her eyes were brimming with pleasure. He smiled knowing full well he had pleased and surprised her. How odd, he thought, that pleasing her would give him so much satisfaction. Her lips just inches away from his were distracting him from all else in the world.

He chuckled. "Haley, might I suggest we get the hell out of the store before I kiss you again. I'm sure I'm breaking some law just standing so close to you."

"Jack," she said softly, "thank you. Thank you so much."

Outside the sun still hung bright in the late afternoon sky and Jack realized he was truly happy. It was Haley and only Haley who was renewing his sense of self. For the first time in too many years he was the man he remembered he was, not a fragment lost in the end of the world.

"Happy?" he asked in a low playful growl.

"Oh yes," she replied leaning into his shoulder. "But you shouldn't have stolen that kiss; I would have given it freely to you had you asked."

"If I were a pirate, Haley, and at the moment I am wishing I was," he said his voice crisp and clean, "I'd take more than a kiss."

Haley laughed and wrapped her arms around him.

"Come on," he said slipping his arm around her waist, "there are still a few things we need to buy."

On their way back to Aunt Molly's Bed and Breakfast, Jack guided Haley into a small boutique.

Jack picked out a white Cuban short sleeve shirt with buttons up the front and a white pair of slacks. Haley picked out a simple clean cut summer dress with spaghetti straps and a pair of light blue sandals.

It was almost six when they returned to their room and reality returned as they neared the Bed and Breakfast. After an almost carefree afternoon, an awkward silence filled the empty space between them. It left her weak and frightened for her sister.

"Jenna should be calling soon," she said nervously.

"Yes," Jack said as he swept her weightless into his arms, "It'll be all right. This will be over soon. You'll have a chance to talk to Jenna and the two of you will straighten this out."

His words sounded hollow to her but they were the right words to say. As if sensing her fears, Jack gently lifted her chin. His breath fanned her face sending a warm shiver through her body; she drowned in his steady gaze.

Her trembling limbs clung to him for safety and he didn't back away.

In a voice that was both soft and sensual as he assured her with soft emphasis, "I said it will be all right."

Haley nodded and stepped into his hard body. She buried her face against his chest and prayed he was right.

He gently rocked her back and forth, aware and oblivious

to everything, except the soft curves of her body. The mere touch of her hand reaching up to his chest sent warming shivers through him.

Try as he could, he couldn't push away the thought of the eight million dollars attached to her. Part of him wished he could will away every cent and just focus on the woman in his arms but the appeal of the millions was too distracting. Buying her the coin and necklace hardly appeased his conscious but the joy and satisfaction of knowing he had made her happy was a gift he had given himself.

God, he swore, why hadn't he met her before Vinnie the Rat came into his life? Why couldn't he have met her when he was in position to give her the world? Why hadn't he met her when he still had a heart to give? His arms encircled her and one hand fell to the delicate small of her back. He felt her eyelashes flutter against his cheek.

It hurt to hold her; it hurt because he realized he was falling in love with her. His heart hammered foolishly at the thought. A woman like her deserved better, yet part of him already knew he was not going to let her go.

In the midst of so much anguish, Haley thought nestling deeper into him, how was it possible to find such a man.

Glamorous, sophisticated beyond her experience, he would never be interested in a small town book store manager, like her. Her emotions were out of control as she realized all the more that she had been thrust upon him and without question or waver, he had accepted her, cared for her and protected her. Would she ever feel this safe again?

The ancient coin buried at sea for hundreds of years pressed against her soft skin. It would always serve as a reminder of him, though she knew she hardly needed a keepsake to hold him in her heart's secret place.

Jenna would be calling soon. This nightmare would be over. Could she dare hope Jack Morgan would still be beside her?

"Hey," he said softly, gently pushing her away.

"Let's change and go grab a bite to eat and catch the sunset at Mallory Square."

Haley nodded.

She retreated into the bathroom, touched up her makeup before changing into her midnight blue summer dress. When she returned to the bedroom, Jack was dressed in his white shirt and slacks. Jack hadn't shaved that morning, his day old beard made him look all the more sensual.

The contrast of his dark hair and bronze skin was striking and she knew she wouldn't be the only woman in Key West giving him a second look.

Jack smiled at the sight of her. The dark blue cotton dress accented her creamy white skin and showed off the graceful lines of her shoulders. Gathered at the waist, the full skirt hung provocatively at the knees and gave him a perfect view of her beautifully shaped calves. Her long dark hair hung in long ringlets that curled on her forehead and on the nape of her neck.

The golden doubloon hung perfectly between the soft mounds of her bodice. He couldn't wait to have her in his arms and would use any excuse he had to keep her there.

On their way back to toward town, Jack stopped and walked quickly to the truck. Haley watched him take something out of the glove compartment and stick in under the shirt. She had forgotten about the gun.

Though the diner next to Aunt Molly's probably offered good food, they chose instead the patio of a seaside restaurant.

Over dinner, they became caught up in the light

conversation that bordered flirtation. Had anyone noticed, they looked like they were falling in love.

Both agreed it was only proper to top their meal with Key Lime pie, which tasted better than it looked and it looked like it had fallen from heaven.

Outside the restaurant, Jack slid his hand down her arm before wrapping around her small hand.

"You know we missed the sunset," he said not sounding sorry.

"I enjoyed the sunset we shared without all the bagpipes, jugglers and crowds." Haley said as they slowly walked down the street.

Jack swung her around and gave her a soft kiss on the lips.

Once again, she noted the soft look in his eyes and could barely breathe as she wondered if his faraway thoughts were for her.

With the sunset celebration long over, most tourists and locals had withdrawn to the bars.

The sound of steel drums and laughter led them to a café where they sat and talked about everything and nothing for the next several hours. Try as she could, as the time approached midnight, Haley grew increasingly nervous.

"It will be over soon," Jack said leaving their waitress a generous tip. "Come on, let's blow this place."

Grateful to accept his arm, they walked about old Key West oblivious to everything and everyone except each other.

Almost eleven-thirty, the cell phone rang.

"I understand," she said to the caller and slipped it back into her dress pocket. With a worried brow, she said, "That was Jenna. She wants us to meet her at the marina now."

They were only two blocks away from the marina and lost little time reaching it.

Multimillion dollar yachts rested comfortably beside sailboat dingys. A light cool breeze was blowing in from Cuba and the stars overhead were glittering against a black velvet sky.

Haley was impatiently looking about. "She said she would be here."

"Give her time," Jack said slowly glancing around. "She'll be here any minute."

In the distance, Haley noticed a young man in a wind breaker skirting around the rigid edges of a building. Hugging the shadows, the teen's brisk pace was purposeful toward the end of the promenade.

It seemed this should be an odd shortcut, Haley thought, but realized they were just one block over from where the streets were filled to capacity with revelries as groups moved from one bar to the next determined to take advantage of the drink specials and the music each offered.

Something about the teen drew her attention as he approached her. A windbreaker and long pants camouflaged his body and a dark baseball cap obscured his face. As Haley watched his purposeful bearing in her direction, she recognized too well the familiar stride, the slight tilt of head and the way he held his arms at his side. Even at this distance, she knew her twin sister.

"Jenna," she said in an excited whisper faintly aware that Jack followed the sound of her words to the stranger approaching them.

Haley rushed to her sister's side and tearfully pulled her into her arms.

Jenna clung to Haley and sobbed. "Haley, I'm so sorry. I'm so sorry."

With her fingers tight on Jenna's shoulder, Haley pushed Jenna to arm's length. In a voice clear that bordered no challenge, she said, "It's all right. We're together. We'll figure this out."

Jack stood speechless watching them. It was disarming to find his beautiful Haley's face so identically duplicated on another woman. Yet, he could instinctively tell them apart.

Though every bit as beautiful, Jack found himself instantly comparing the twins. Jenna was as striking as Haley but she lacked her gentle nature. Jack sensed Jenna would fold during a crisis while Haley, his Haley, in spite of her softness, would hold her ground like a badger for someone she loved. His heart twisted realizing he wanted that love.

"Who's this?" Jenna asked noticing him for the first time. "Is he a Marshall?"

Haley looked over her perfectly sculptured shoulder to Jack and smiled.

"No," Haley said turning back to her sister, "he's not a Marshall or FBI. His name is Jack Morgan and he's someone we can trust."

Suspicious and in near panic, Jenna whispered loud enough for Jack to hear. "Does he know about the money?"

"Yes," came Haley's quick reply.

"You shouldn't have told him," Jenna scolded. "You shouldn't have told anyone."

"Like it's a secret?" Haley snapped. "Trust me; I was the last to find out about the money, Jenna. I said nothing to the Marshals about you leaving me in the middle of this mess. Furthermore, your boyfriend sent a bunch of thugs to the safe house. Men died so I could escape. Jack gave me a safe place to stay but Carlos and Diego found us there. They blew up Jack's home and business. You need to understand Jenna, I owe, we owe, this man our lives."

"Oh my god," Jenna sobbed. "Haley, I'm so sorry. They assured me that I would be entirely safe."

Tears began streaming down Jenna's face. "Oh Haley, I am so sorry, I would have never involved you in all this."

"Never mind that now," Haley said keeping her voice smooth but insistent. "Now, you need to tell me, tell us, how this happened? Why are you running from Ricky? Why did you steal eight million dollars from a drug cartel?"

Jenna pulled away from Haley's arms and sat at a wired bench nearest them. Her shoulders slumped and her voice was barely audible as she began, "Life was so good last winter, Haley. My modeling had really taken off. Then I met Ricky."

"The Angel of Death," Jack interjected and for which he earned a hard glare from both twins.

"Go on," Haley urged her sister.

"Ricky told me he was in the import-export business. I'm not as smart as you, Haley. I didn't think to at what he was doing and when I found out, it was too late. Knowing everything I do about him now, I still love him and he loves me but I also knew I had to get away from him and his life."

"Why?" Haley pressed her. "Why would you ever leave someone you love?"

"I had to, Haley. I just grabbed the money and ran but you've got to believe, I have no intention of testifying against Ricky, I just wanted to get away. I thought the U.S. Marshals would help me."

Jack nearly choked at her naivety. "It doesn't work that way, Jenna. And if I may, that's a heck of a lot of money to walk out the door with."

"They were in bearer bonds and in an attaché case," Jenna explained. There was a faint tremor of regret in her voice. "I only wanted to use it as leverage to get away."

Haley took a step toward her. "Why do you need leverage?"

Jenna looked down and sobbed. "Because, because I'm pregnant."

"You're pregnant?" Haley cried in surprise. "Oh my God, Jenna! Does, Ricky know?"

"No, and he can never find out. I don't want my baby becoming…"

"Like his father," Jack finished for her.

"Where are the bonds now?" Haley asked.

"They're in a safe deposit box in the Bahamas. I had planned on giving back the money to Ricky in the hopes he would let me go but when I called him, he was furious. He warned me his brother had put a contact out on my head; that's when I called in the FBI. Haley, I know how stupid this sounds but I do love Ricky and I don't want to hurt him. He's the father of my child. I thought if I had a few days I could sort all this out."

Haley frowned. "Is that when you called me?"

"Yes, but I thought the FBI was going to take you to a safe house. I thought you would be safe there and I was worried about you too. I don't think Ricky would hurt you but I'm not sure about his family. His brother Luis is horrible."

"You said the bonds are in the Bahamas?"

Jenna looked down at the ground. "Yes, they are in a safety deposit box. Oh Haley, I'm such a fool. I have no choice now. I've to go to the FBI or the U.S. Marshals, whoever; I have to get out of this."

"You fell in love with a dangerous man," Haley said coming

to sit beside her sister. "Don't worry, we'll figure something out."

Jack shifted, drawing the attention of the sister. "We have another problem, Jenna; someone in the Marshall's office gave you up."

"Oh my God," Jenna said clutching Haley. "Who?"

Haley stood to join him. Too late, Jack saw the silhouette of man with an assault rifle rise from one of the boats and point the gun directly at Haley. He screamed as the mussel fire exploded in the darkness.

Pushing her out of its path, the bullet passed her.

Jenna screamed and fell to the ground. Blood splatter colored the cement.

"Get down!" Jack screamed. Positioning himself between the sisters, he pulled Billy Two Bears gun from under the back of his shirt and returned two shots.

"Cease fire!" a dark male voice called out over the blast of gunfire. Even with the barrage, they could hear the metallic snap of guns prepared to shoot. "This is the FBI! You're under arrest!"

Haley crawled the distance to Jenna and sheltered her body with her own. Looking up at Haley, Jenna said, "Oh my god, I'm going to die."

"You're not going to die," Haley said her voice low and smooth. "You are going to live."

"Take this," Jenna said pulling the chain with the bank key from around her neck. "Take the money and run, Haley. Get out of here. Do you still have the cell?"

Blood was freely flowing from her shoulder. Jenna looked at Jack. "Will you take care of her?"

Jack gave Jenna one nod of his head. Jenna smiled. So, she thought looking at her sister, Haley had found love, too.

The gun fire stopped; the silence was deafening.

"Jack Morgan, Jenna Rollins," the man behind the bull horn bellowed out to them, "Stay where you are!"

First in English then Spanish, an order was made for the men in the boat to drop their weapons and rise. Under the explosive lights of the Coast Guard vessel that came barreling into the marina from the dark waters, the men did just that.

As the armed FBI and SWAT Team moved in, Jenna looked up, her eyes fading and her voice unnatural, she said, "Listen to me. Ricky is not going to give up, Haley. Our only chance is to get the money and get it back to him."

Haley cradled her sister and Jenna whispered the name of the bank into her ear.

"No," Haley cried in protest. "I'm not leaving you!"

The FBI was upon them.

Jack rose slightly showing his gun to the approaching agent. He then laid it on the ground and stepped away from it, his hands high in the air.

"My sister has been shot!" Haley screamed in outrage.

"Get an ambulance," the agent called out.

"Jenna!" Haley screamed.

Jenna looked up and gave Haley a soft smile. Jenna pressed a small safety deposit key into Haley's palm and closed her fingers tight about it.

"Haley," she said in a dark whisper, "Get out of here. Get the money. Give it back to Ricky. It's our only chance!"

CHAPTER NINE

In a voice that was velvet edged and strong, Jack said, "She's right, Haley. The Feds won't be able to keep you or your sister safe. Your only chance is to return the money."

Hot tears burned Haley's face. "I'm not leaving my sister!"

Jenna's fingers tightened around Haley's hand. "Haley, do this! Please! The FBI will take care of me and my baby. Right now, everyone still thinks you're Jenna Rollins. Let them. Get out of here. Get back to Miami. Call Ricky. Return the money. It may not stop what is meant to be but at least it will buy us some time."

Haley shook her head. "No. I'm not leaving you."

Jenna looked at Jack. She was street savvy and this was a man who knew the streets. "Get her out of here!"

Jack didn't hesitate. He had no choice. He had no more time. With the paramedics racing toward them, he lifted Haley to her feet. Drawing her back into his arms, he held her. Beneath him, he felt her wretched little spirit straining forward, ready to fall back upon her sister. Before she could twist away from him, the paramedics reached Jenna.

"Who's she?" the uniformed SWAT Commander demanded as he joined them.

Crumbled on the ground, Jenna looked up; her eyes steadfast on Haley.

"She's my younger sister," Haley sobbed and watched Jenna's lips curve into a soft smile.

"They'll take care of her," the SWAT Commander snapped. His cold impersonal voice was filled with reproach as he turned to Jack. "I assume you're Jack Morgan. Take Miss Rollins to the vehicles and wait there. We're under orders to get you two back to Miami."

Jack squeezed Haley to silence. Ignoring him, Haley glared at the Commander. Her little jaw squared in defiance and she met his icy gaze straight on. "No."

"You have two choices, Miss Rollins," the Commander barked. "You can go willingly or you can go cuffed. Pick one! A helicopter is waiting for you. You'll be taken to a safe place."

Been there, done that, Haley wanted to spit at his face. Above the paramedics' heads, Jenna mouthed "go."

"Your sister is in good hands, Jenna," Jack said tightening his grip on her elbow. "Let's do what the nice officer said."

Pulling her forcibly away from her twin proved more difficult than he imagined. Haley fought every step of the way and he had to push her through the throng of heavily armed law enforcement officers who had gathered at the marina. Haley kept looking back over her shoulders but Jack forced her to keep moving forward.

How had the FBI found them? At the moment he didn't care. His one thought was to get Haley out of danger and leave Jenna to the care of paramedics.

Pushing her down the dock, they could hear SWAT Team shouting loud directives at the yacht. The Columbians were being taken into custody.

Jack and Haley met with little resistance as they weaved their way toward the streets. The local sheriff deputies and Key West police officers who stood about the squad cars and armored vehicles barely noticed them as the Rojas assassins were taken into custody at the marina.

Jerking free from him, Haley turned on Jack. "How could you?"

"Because I can," he snapped.

Hot tears spilled down her cheeks. "My sister may be dying."

"You sister will be fine, Haley. There's nothing you can do but return the money to Ricky Rojas. Come on," Jack said his hand sliding down her arm to her wrist. "We've got to get out of here."

Yanking her wrist, he took the lead and pulled her toward the late night party goers who had gathered behind the police barricades.

"Hey," a Key West police officer yelled out at them as they slipped into the crowd. "You aren't supposed to be across the line."

Jack waved in apology and scooted Haley to the far edge of the crowd. Haley yanked back and stopped Jack in his tracks.

"Why are you doing this?" she shouted. "Tell me why!"

"Why what, Haley?" He said sweeping her into his arms. "Why I am I keeping you out of harm's way? Why I'm still here? Why do I want to keep you safe?"

He looked down at her. His face softened as he studied her beautiful face. Then surprising even himself, he said, "Because I'm falling in love you."

He watched as the heavy lashes that shadowed her cheeks flew up. Astonishment touched her pale tear stained face and she looked more uncertain than ever.

Drawing a hard breath, he knew the FBI was probably aware they had slipped away. He couldn't afford one moment to kiss those delicious full lips. Instead he smiled and said softly. "Now right now, you stubborn little twit, we need to leave Key West and get to Miami. COME ON!"

Haley refused to move. Surprised by his confession, he knew he was losing valuable time. "Honey, don't fight me every step of the way."

Jack searched her face for understanding. "I didn't see Carlos and Diego on the boat; that means they could be around here right now. We've got to leave! Your sister's life depends on it. Damn it, Haley; your life depends on it!"

The truth sucked the air from her lungs. Jack was right. Jenna was right. She had to get to the money. With it, she could barter for her sister's life.

"All right," Haley cried. "Let's get out of Key West before they close the island."

Jack grinned and grabbed her hand. Willingly, Haley ran with him through the dark streets toward Aunt Molly's Bed and Breakfast and to Billy Two Bears' battered truck.

"Anything we need in the room?" Jack called out to her.

Haley shook her head.

Jack jumped in the Chevy. "Get in!"

Overhead the street lights seemed to dance and sway in the night's soft breeze. Party goers were crisscrossing across the streets at the north end of the island unaware of the events unfolding at the marina.

With his fingers hard on the steering wheel, he drove down the dark side streets through a small residential neighborhood of white framed houses and apartments. Returning to U.S. 1, he pressed his foot on the accelerator and headed north. Haley said nothing, allowing Jack to focus on the drive.

Looking out into the darkness, she caught glimpses of the wave and water. Houses, small surf shops and public and private marines were obscured in dark outlines. She dared not return to the moment when he said he had loved her. Still too stunned to respond, she allowed herself a private and secret smile and knew even in the darkness of the truck her eyes sparkled with a fierce light. This was not the time to tell him she loved him too.

It took them an hour to reach Big Pine Key. Jack glanced at his watch; it would be another two and a half hours before they reached Miami. In Miami, they could get lost in the mean streets but with only one road in and out of the Keys, they were vulnerable and exposed each mile of the way.

Jack drove wordless through the Lower Keys toward Marathon.

"No one seems to be looking for us," Haley said at last with an anxious glance over her shoulder.

"Yeah," Jack said with a glance in his rearview mirror. "We should've hit a road block by now. I can think of only one explanation; Jenna told the Marshals who she was. They no longer care about us, Haley. It's the only reason why we haven't been stopped by now."

"Why would she do that?" Haley asked looking back to Jack.

He grinned feeling somewhat relieved. "To keep you safe. I'm sure the Feds are keeping that information to themselves. Did Jenna tell you where she hid the bonds?"

"Hamilton Bank on Grand Bahama Island."

Eight million dollars at his fingertips, he thought with a smile.

Haley shifted slightly. "How do we get in touch with Ricky?"

Jack choked on his laugh. "That shouldn't be too hard. You may be safe from the Feds, sweetie, but you're in the cross hairs of the Rojas Cartel."

Trying to focus her attention on the long dark stretch of highway ahead of them, Haley drew a soft breath. "At least Jenna is safe."

Jack gassed up the truck in Saddlebunch Keys, brought cold sodas and a bag of chips. Back on U.S. 1, he adjusted the rear view mirror and glanced at Haley's lovely profile. "I can't believe how you and Jenna look alike. And I'm not sure I've ever seen adult twins."

Haley laughed. "I suppose it can be a bit of a surprise. I told you we were identical."

"I could tell you apart." He said with unexpected tenderness.

Haley blushed and looked out as they passed another mile marker. She was another mile from her sister and the guilt of leaving her clung to her like a second skin. "I'm worried about Jenna."

"Don't be!" Jack said shifting slightly in his seat. "She'll be fine."

"Oh and how do you know?" Haley questioned him softly.

"I've been shot before honey. It hurts like hell but she'll live."

"You weren't pregnant."

"Don't worry, Haley, I'm sure she will be fine," Jack said as they began crossing the Seven Mile Bridge.

"Oh my God," Haley said with a soft smile. "Jenna's going to be a Mother and I'm going to be an aunt."

Jack's lips curled into a soft smile seeing the wonder in Haley's face. "Try to get some rest. Tomorrow isn't going to be any easier."

Haley shyly leaned into him and he gently brought his arm over her. She curled into his body. The fit was perfect.

Jack was right. Jenna was getting the best of care. She frowned and prayed that she and the baby were alright. With the dreamy thought of seeing Jenna again, holding her niece or nephew in her arms, Haley closed her eyes, and allowed the steady purr of the truck's motor to lull her to sleep.

She awoke with a sudden start, instantly awake and surprised to find the Chevy parked in front of a motel.

"Oh my gosh," she said rising from the seat. "Where are we? What time is it?"

"Miami," Jack said stretching his arms. "And it's late."

Haley shook off her sleep. "I guess I was poor company."

Jack grinned. "Actually it was kinda nice having you curled up next to me."

Haley blushed. "Oh sure, with me sleeping? Did I snore?"

Jack grinned. "I'm going in and getting us a room."

Haley got out of the truck. Feeling slightly rested, it felt good to stretch her legs. In what seemed like minutes, Jack was back at her side.

"We can leave the truck where it is. Our room is up on the second floor. Come on, sleepy head."

Climbing the stairs after him, Haley grabbed onto the railing. "You've been wonderful, Jack. Thank you. I'm not sure Jenna and I deserve your help. I don't know how I can ever repay you."

"Well, I can understand how you feel that way," Jack drawled with sarcasm. "I'm such a catch especially now that I don't even have that dump of a hellhole anymore."

Haley paused at the top of the open stairwell. "We could rebuild."

Jack turned and stared at her. His expression grew stilled. "Yeah, that would be nice."

Watching him, Haley noted his set jaw, his clamped mouth and the curious heart rendering tenderness in his dark brown eyes. He looked her over seductively and her heart turned in response. Turning from her, he slipped the key into the door.

The door opened to a clean little room with a floral bedspread atop the double bed. The room was dark, inviting. Jack walked to the bathroom and hit the light switch; a soft light swept quietly into the room. Haley entered and closed the door.

Jack looked back at her, to find her still standing by the door. Her luminous blue eyes smoldered with a fire that burned into his soul.

As her soft lips curled into a faint smile, he stood quietly, intoxicated by her beauty. A knot in his stomach tightened and he reminded himself to breath. Captivated by her, he said simply, "Haley."

Across from him, Haley's heart jumped at the sound of her name. Jack's body was perfectly silhouetted against the light. His powerful masculine frame was overwhelming and filled every dark corner of the room. She could feel his breath caressing her and he had yet to pull her into his arms. A lightening storm of emotions sent her spinning into the dark underworld of her soul and she knew. She knew she was lost to him and he hadn't even crossed the room. Her heart swelled. He meant to claim her. She lowered her eyes in surrender.

Coming to her side, Jack swept her weightlessly into his arms; his mouth covered hers in delicious pleasure. His fingers were at the nape of her neck, sweeping up into the thick mat of her rich brown hair.

Haley's arms circled his waist, pulling him closer and allowing her soft curves to mold into the contours of his lean body. She returned his kiss, lost in her own hunger, drugged by his desire.

His lips left her mouth burning with fire as they slowly

floated just above her skin to nibble at a small soft earlobe before searing a path down her neck to her shoulders. Waves of ecstasy throbbed through her with each gentle twist of his mouth.

His fingers moved delightfully to the spaghetti straps and with a feather touch slipped them off her silken shoulders allowing them to fall loosely about her arms. With searing heat, he covered her mouth with demanding mastery and fresh urgency.

Her body pressed into his, her arms wrapped around his neck as his arms encircled her. In one fluid movement, he swept her into his arms lifting her as if she were weightless.

In his arms, Haley buried her face in the corded muscles of his chest. In long strides, he crossed the room, and gently laid her atop the bed.

Unable to steady her heart's rhythm, Haley felt warm blood coursing through her veins like an awakened river.

As he laid her back upon the bed, her hand slid forward to his shirt and felt him shake as her small fingers eagerly unbuttoned his shirt. His hands pressed into the bed to keep from falling onto her and he pushed himself to her side.

"I don't want to hurt you," he said between heavy breaths. Warming shivers fanned her skin. Haley smiled softly. Her heart hammered in her chest. "You will never hurt me, Jack."

"I swear," he said his voice choking with emotion, "I'll never hurt you or see you harmed."

His powerful hand found her silken thigh and slide up to the soft curve of her hip. His knee pushed between her smooth inner thighs opening them. Willingly, she gave way to his powerful legs and heard him moan as his fingers found the velvet softness between her legs.

His lips were once again upon her, drinking in her

sweetness as fresh currents of desire transported him to a spiraling furrow of deepening pleasure.

Haley arched her back pushing her body into his. Her small hand danced across his hard chest to his shoulders before pushing his shirt away from his shoulder. Encumbered by the weight of the light shirt, Jack rose and ripped the shirt from his back. His fingers slipped into the top of her dress, pulling it to her waist exposing her beautiful full white breasts.

Blood pounded in her brain and her knees trembled as his hand burned its way from her waist to her upper thighs taking her dress with it. She lifted her hips and was rewarded with a light caress to her soft round bottom.

"You're so beautiful," he cried as his mouth came down on one perfectly shaped nipple.

She stroked the strong muscles of his back as his hand pushed the last of her dress and her soft silken panties from her body. She lay naked beneath him, her nipples rigid in the cool air conditioned room.

He gently eased down to her body, his hands capturing her breasts, cupping them, kneading her breasts as his tongue moved from side to side sucking them until she felt as if she would explode in pleasure.

"Jack," Haley cried as his hands began exploration of her soft flesh. She lay panting, her body neatly tucking closer to his hard body.

For one brief moment, his hands left her and she felt the brief rush of his pants slide down her exposed legs before falling to the floor.

Naked beside her, he gently leaned into the sensual length of her body. She gasped as his bare chest touched her nipples. Her body was on fire and she breathed in deep soul drenching drafts of wanton desire. She writhed beneath him; her breasts tingled against his rough chest.

Taking her hand, he brought it to his lips and kissed the palm before guiding it to the throbbing hardness between his legs.

At the touch of her fingers his body shook and his breath became long shallow moans as erotic pleasure coursed through him. He was long, hard and could feel the shivers of delight with each gentle stroke of her fingers.

Aroused to the peak of desire, she led his manhood into her soft warm opening and cried out in pleasure as he slid into her. Together they began to move in a symphony of pleasure. Their bodies found the tempo that of exquisite harmony. Involuntary tremors of pleasure rocked Haley with each drive of his hips.

A moan of ecstasy slipped through her lips and her body arched and rose to meet him in uncontrolled passion.

Through a delicious fog of hungry desire, she heard him say, ""Haley, honey, I can't wait…"

Exhilarated by his possession, Haley shattered into a million glowing stars.

"Now!" she cried as bursting sensations of pleasure rushed through her. Spiraling into a glorious web of crazed passion, she heard his cry of surrender. Each tiny explosion sent new waves of ecstasy through her and she lay drowning in the floodtide of sensual delight. She gasped in sweet agony as he fell upon her.

For a moment, she laid still, her body radiating in unspeakable pleasure. He fell from her and smiled.

"I'm sorry, I should have…"

"Hush," she said, "I found my pleasure, my love."

"Was it sweet, angel?" he asked, his hands still hungrily reaching for her body.

Haley smiled sweetly leaving him no room for doubt. "Yes, Jack, it was sweet, very sweet."

"Tomorrow, I'll give you endless pleasure," he promised. With one indelible kiss, exhausted from their lovemaking, from the long drive, from the anxiety of the day, he was instantly asleep in her arms.

Haley snuggled closer. She never thought his arms around her still could feel so warm, so gentle. She smiled.

Somewhere in the night the waves of the Atlantic caressed the sand. At one with the motion of all life, Haley felt her eyelids lower and allowed herself to sleep.

She woke in his arms the next morning and gently slipped out of his arms. She stood just a moment looking at his handsome face full of strength, shining in the dim morning light with a serene peace she had never seen before. In sleep, he reached out to where she had lay beside him. A scowl shadowed his brow as his hands moved across the warm sheets until he found her pillow. He pulled it to him and tucked it under his arms. Neatly held, the restless stirring ceased and he returned to a deeper sleep.

Haley smiled remembering his masterful seduction. With a pleasant ache, she went to the bathroom and washed her face. The digital clock had read 10:35 AM. Jack would be waking soon. He had surprised her with coffee the other morning, she could do no less.

Dressing quickly she looked at the woman in the mirror and knew maintaining his strength happily fulfilled her self-serving agenda. She lifted twenty dollars from the dresser and grabbed the room key.

The morning was glorious even in this warehouse district.

Sea gulls flew high over head against a beautiful light blue sky. Haley never felt happier as she passed the maid with a laundry cart.

Across the street from the motel, a busy truck stop was already busy with customers. She knew she would find coffee and food there. She would be returning to his arms soon enough she thought, her lips still burning with his kisses.

A hostess at the Circle J Truck Stop took her order and in less than five minutes she was walking through the parking lot with two cups of coffee and two Sunrise Specials.

Crossing the street, she barely took notice of a sleek black sedan, among the big rigs. Intent on not spilling the coffee and keeping their breakfast plates upright, she didn't pay attention as it moved up closer on her.

Passing Billy's beat up truck, the aroma of hot biscuits, and bacon rose from the bag she was carrying reminding her of her hunger. Jack would be hungry for more than breakfast.

As she was about to climb the steps to the second floor, she was jerked backwards. Coffee spilled across her hand. The bagged breakfast fell at her feet. She tried to scream but a rough hand covered her mouth.

"Good Morning, Miss Jenna," Carlos hissed into her ear. "If you scream, I will slit your lovely throat. You are no longer under his protection. Jenna. By the way, Luis his brother has flown up from Bogotá. So many people are not happy with you. So, come quietly and we will not kill your boyfriend in front of you. Do you understand?"

With his hand hard on her mouth, Haley nodded. She recoiled in horror, a cold fist closing over her heart.

"Don't scream," Carlos warned her as he slowly removed his hand from her mouth. "Good. See, I told Diego, she would be nice this time."

Gulping for air, she stared at him in numbed horror.

Carlos eyes raked her with open fury. With an arrogant twist of his mouth, his face hardened into a mask of hatred. He shoved a gun into her side and pushed her hard into the street.

On cue, the sleek sedan pulled up beside them and the back door swung open. Diego slid across the seat and motioned for Carlos to shove her in. He did.

A dark skinned heavy set driver smirked as Diego pulled her further into the car.

Carlos slid in beside her; her skin crawled at his contact. He laid his arm behind her and smiled. To the driver he said, "Get us out of here!"

The driver nodded and jammed the gear shift hard as he pulled out of the parking lot.

Ricky had found her; Haley thought her stomach knotting in apprehension.

She would have to think fast.

In the motel room, Jack woke slowly. Pushing the pillow he was holding off the bed, he looked to the light glowing from the bathroom.

"Oh man," he said with a yawn then called out to her. "I slept like a rock. How about bringing your cute little ass back to bed?"

No answer. Sensing something was wrong; Jack rose and pushed back the covers. "Haley?"

In two steps, he left the bed and stared into the empty bathroom.

"What the hell?" he said looking to the dresser. He noticed the money scattered across the top of the bureau. She had taken some money but the truck key was still there. Had she gone for coffee? He thought with a growing sense of alarm.

Grabbing his pants, he rushed out of the motel room, half expecting her to be walking toward him with two cups of coffee.

Below him, he watched a black sedan skid from the truck stop and slide to a stop just below him. Too late, he understood.

"HALEY!" he screamed as Carlos savagely pushed her into the backseat. Blood drained from his body as he watched Carlos slam the car door. The sedan whirled about the parking lot spraying gravel in its thunderous escape.

Running back into the room, Jack snatched the truck keys from the dresser. He ran barefoot out to the cement balcony and down the single flight of stairs.

Ignoring the sting of rock beneath his feet, he yanked open the truck door and slid into the seat.

"Come on, damm it," he shrieked twisting the key into the ignition. The engine's scream ricocheted through him. Without glancing back, Jack jammed the Chevy into reverse and grabbed the swinging driver door, slamming it shut.

Hitting the clutch and first gear, he floored the gas pedal. Sending gravel through the air around him, he drove the Chevy into the street, cutting off a white delivery truck.

Ignoring the loud blast of the horn, Jack jerked the wheel too fast nearly sending him into a passing SUV. He jerked the wheel right and steadied the truck. Up shifting in brutal savagery, he drove past a delivery, around a semi taking most of the road for a turn before running a red light.

Miraculously, he spotted the sedan, a half mile ahead of him making a left turn. Each breath he took pushed him faster forward, his body twisting with each turn of the wheel, frantic to reach her. He took the turn fast, nearly hitting a forklift backing into the street. Swerving across the road, he maneuvered about the forklift; his attention refocused on finding the sedan.

Halfway down the block, he slammed his fist on the steering wheel. "DAMM IT TO HELL!"

Breath was raw in his throat and his body shook with rage. Haley was gone.

Slamming on the brakes, the Chevy came to a screeching halt. Jack stared down the road damning her kidnappers to hell and back. For Ricky Rojas, he had one message and he angrily screamed it out. "ROJAS, COUNT YOUR FRIGGIN' LIFE IN MINUTES! YOU'RE A DEAD MAN."

CHAPTER TEN

Inside the sedan, Haley sent Diego a warning look. His mercurial black eyes sharpened and his fat buttery brown lips curled as if on the edge of laughter. If he thought she was defenseless, he would find himself mistaken she vowed.

Blazing with sudden fury, all she wanted in life at that moment was to wipe that smile from his face. Seeing the subtle look of hesitation in his eyes, she felt a sudden surge of triumph. How ever he thought to harm her, she saw the reluctance. He halted just as he reached the edge of reason.

She forced herself to remain calm; despite his audacity, he would not harm her. She saw it in his eyes. Haley could only image the consequences of striking Ricky Rojas's woman.

"Do not think for one minute you can manhandle me you Columbian pig," she hissed mustering up as much indignation as she could manage. "Touch me again and you're a dead man."

Diego laughed nervously. "Did you hear this whore, Carlos?" he said looking to his companion. Turning back to her he said, "You are es-a stupid, Jenna."

He grinned exposing his gold front teeth. "I told you, Luis is here, you know, Ricky's brother. Women like you are nothing to him. Nothing. You are dirt to his feet."

Haley narrowed her eyes. "PIG!" she spat at him and looked ahead.

"Don't pay attention to him Jenna." Carlos said with

a conspiratorial wink to Diego. "He's just excited because he thinks Luis will give us the pleasure of your company tonight."

"Don't be ridiculous," Haley said trying to keep her voice from trembling. "Do you imagine for one minute Ricky would let..."

Carlos turned on her, his black eyes bulging from their sockets. He moved his heavy body closer to her. In a soft whisper, his mouth twisted. "I suppose you don't know then?"

"Know what?" Haley demanded. She was becoming increasingly unnerved by his scrutiny.

"Ricky is dead."

"No," Haley cried in a startled gasp. Jenna's lover, her protector, dead? She tried to keep her hands from shaking. Swallowing hard she knew she could not show fear. A terrible apprehension spread through her body, sending icy shards through her blood vessels. Her thoughts should have been for her own safety but she shuddered inwardly, thinking of the anguish Jenna would suffer when she learned the father of her child was dead. She felt a nauseating wave of revulsion spread through her. Closing her eyes; her heart ached for Jenna's pain.

She held her silence. Was this true? Could this be real? Behind closed lids, she thought of Jack still sleeping at the motel and wondered if she would be dead before he even woke. She tightened her lids as she remembered the strain in Jack's voice when he said he loved her.

At the moment she could do nothing, wedged between two gun wielding Columbian thugs who would like nothing better to do at the moment than to slit her throat; she couldn't afford the luxury of feeling fear or knowing love. Girding herself with resolve, she would have to rely on her wits to stay alive. With a passion to stay alive if only to see Jack one more time, she felt blood pounding its way through her chest.

Think, think, she demanded. Think. Reason like a lost friend returned, and she remembered she had several momentary advantages. First, she wasn't Jenna; second, she knew where the money was and last, she was prepared to return the eight million to the Rojas Drug Lords in exchange for her life. Surely, this counted for something.

Drawing a deep breath, she slowly opened her eyes and realized she was on Interstate 95 headed north. Where were they taking her? Presumably to Luis Rojas. Sinking her fingernails into the palm of her hands to steady her spiraling emotions she struggled to prepare herself for what was to happen next but her thoughts returned to Jack.

Ignoring Diego and Carlos, she focused her attention on the fast moving traffic around the sedan. Her thoughts returned to Jack.

He would be as she left him, sleeping, she thought. Her heart was pounding erratically. I should have told him; she thought with regret. Her heart cried out to him, why didn't I tell you when I had the chance that I was in love with you too.

She bit her lip to keep from crying. I can't think of Jack now, she told herself but in her mind's eye, she thought of Jack waking. Would he search the room? Call out her name? Would he come for her?

A firm warning voice reminded her that hope would rob her of precious time, time she needed to prepare herself for Luis Rojas. She had been prepared to speak to Ricky. She was not prepared to meet with his brother.

At that moment, the heavy set driver changed lanes. He was taking the exit to Key Biscayne.

Of course, she thought, they were going to the marina, to Ricky's yacht. She tried to bring back memories of Ricky's yacht. Jenna had given her the grand tour but it seemed a lifetime ago. Still, she forced herself to remember every detail. She glanced at the watch on Diego's wrist. They would be at the marina inside of twenty minutes. Twenty minutes would not give her much time to plan an escape if Luis rejected her offer.

She tried to push down the fearful images that were forming inside her. It would be easy for Luis Rojas to take her on board, murder her then drop her body in the warm waters of the Gulf Stream.

Across town, Jack had returned to the motel. He searched for the sedan another fifteen minutes before he admitted he lost the car. At a breakneck speed, he returned to the motel with only one thought in his mind: to find her.

"Hell no," he screamed into the phone. Fear and anger knotted inside him. The ferocity of his hatred was escalating as his fingers turned white from his grip on the phone. Sheer black fright swept through him. "Hell no, I didn't get the damm license number. They pulled out of the parking lot too fast and I never got close enough to read the number."

At the other end of the call, Jack heard Frank's heavy sigh of reproach. "Did you see who took her?"

"What the fuck? Who the hell do you think took her, you asshole?" Jack cussed angrily into the phone.

Jack listened to silence, bridling his anger. Before he could say more, Frank cleared his throat and steadied his voice. "Jack, I want you to calm down. We both have a lot riding on this. Now, let's walk through this, Jack."

Jack narrowed his eyes and the knot in his stomach begged

for release but Frank was right; he would need a cool head if he were going to find Haley and find her he would.

"Okay," Frank began in a lower, huskier voice, "We have agents stationed outside the Rojas compound in Ft. Lauderdale. There's been no unusual activity there though we have had a report that Luis Rojas might have entered the country. Trust me; every federal agent in South Florida is on the lookout for Luis, he makes El Angel de la Morte, look like a saint..."

Frank paused and let out a long audible breath before continuing. "Okay, there is a yacht. Maybe..."

The muscles of his forearm hardened beneath his sleeve. THE YACHT! Haley told him about her lunch with Ricky and Jenna aboard the yacht. Luis sure as hell could have slipped into the U.S. on a private yacht. Ricky would be there with his brother, waiting, waiting for Haley. Jack's nostrils flared with fury; the stakes were higher and the price of Haley's life doubled.

"Jack," Frank spoke with cool resolve, "I want you to remain where you are. I'll..."

The line went dead leaving Frank to stare blankly at the phone.

Jack was already out the door, running down the steps toward the Chevy.

"Like hell I'm going to wait for your dumb ass," he said jumping into the truck. Within minutes he had maneuvered the Chevy onto Interstate 95. He didn't want to think a thought beyond reaching Biscayne Bay.

The sedan pulled up beside a glistening white yacht. Stem to stern it was more impressive than Haley remembered; and more threatening.

Diego stepped out of the car first and motioned for Haley to follow. She slid across the seat and stepped out in front of the sleek gangway. His eyes were black, cold and reminded her of a slow moving shark. She swept past him and looked up at the two hundred foot yacht.

Everything came back to her as she remembered in detail the sundeck with its fashionable full bar, elegant table, chairs, and private lounge. The upper deck housed the main saloon with priceless Columbian artifacts, expensive furniture, a formal dining room, small theater style cinema, gymnasium and Ricky's office. The dining area was linked to the entertainment area by a fashionable rotunda.

The main deck boasted five queen size guest cabins all with Italian marble tile in the bathrooms, flat screen TVs and luxurious furnishings including queen size beds, mahogany dressers and end tables and full size closets. The fifteen man crew and the yacht's powerful engines occupied the lower deck.

Haley made a quick scan of her surroundings. Midday, there was little to no activity about this side of the exclusive marina aside from a delivery man who was carrying boxes on board a seventy-two foot sport fisherman. He paid them no mind, and why should he? She would certainly find no one to help her once aboard the luxury cruiser.

As if to read her thought, Carlos came up behind her, his breath rancid on her neck. "Don't bother screaming, Jenna," he said with lethal calmness, "no on is going to save you."

With burning and reproachful eyes, Haley glared at him, her bright mockery invading his stare. He clenched his mouth tighter and she tossed her hair across her shoulders in a gesture of defiance. She lifted her chin and boldly met his challenge. "Don't think for one minute I'm afraid of you," she boasted, "you'll be licking the bottom of my heels before the day is through."

Carlos grunted and to her complete surprise, smiled. "You have not lost your fire, Jenna. Good, you will need it when I come to your cabin tonight."

She colored fiercely and her body stiffened. Before she could offer him a sharp retort, he said, "Come on, Luis is waiting."

Contempt for both men forbade further argument and she was simply too furious to speak. Anger and alarm rippled along her spine. Did they even imagine she would allow them to touch her?

She shook with impotent rage and fear knowing her life and the life of her sister might very well hang in the balance. Stay calm, she told herself. With her legs heavy but knowing she had no choice but to move forward, she slowly climbed the gangway with Diego in front of her and Carlos behind. She looked down at the dark water between the dock and the yacht. She could jump but her chances of survival were slim. She had to talk to Luis if she were to live to see sunset. She had to make him listen. There was for her no other option.

On the main deck, Diego turned to the bow and climbed a staircase to the upper deck. Haley had no choice but to follow him.

Entering the main salon, she saw a tall man standing with his back to her staring out of the yacht's picture windows.

"Hello Jenna," Luis said turning slowly in her direction. His English wasn't as polished as Ricky's. His voice was cold, hard and she knew this man was not to be played with. As he turned to face her a satanic smile spread across his lips.

Luis was not quite six foot tall, with brilliant liquid black eyes and a handsome face that was still and serious. Holding a rock glass with dark liquid, he walked toward her and smiled benignly as if he were dealing with a temperamental child.

Dressed in a black silk shirt which was open to his chest

and black trousers, he moved like a jungle cat toward her. His skin was taut over the elegant ridge of his cheekbones and he was well groomed, polished and possessed the elegance of a millionaire playboy. No one would suspect that he was a drug lord and a murderer.

Haley took a seat across from him.

"Nice to see you again, my dear," he said. His black eyes were startling against his bronze skin.

Haley felt the knot in her stomach harden. He said "again." Oh God, Jenna had met him. When? What did she know of him? Worse, what did he know of her?

"And Jenna," he said, capturing her with his eyes, "you look cheap and shabby, not so beautiful, not so high and mighty."

Haley rolled her eyes at him. The last thing on her mind was her dress. "I could care less about your opinion of me," she spat back. Her eyes managed to tear but not for the reason he would have thought. "Is Ricky dead?"

Luis stared at her. His eyes were intense, hooded like those of a hawk. "So, you do love my brother. I can see it in your eyes. This creates a problem for me."

Haley looked down at the floor. "Why should my feelings cause you any problems, Luis?"

"You see, you stole from my family and that can't go unpunished. It would look bad for business. You understand?"

Haley looked back at him and shifted in her seat. Forcing images of Jack and Jenna from her mind, she had forgotten she should be afraid. Still, she thought hiding her smile, she had achieved one small victory. Luis had fallen for her masquerade. Whatever he did or was about to do, he'd believe he was doing to Jenna. Her sister would be safe.

Luis took a slip of his drink and gave her a boldly raking

gaze. "First, I should tell you Ricky is not dead. He's alive and will be back shortly."

"How could you tell me such a lie?" Haley screamed in anger.

Luis chuckled. "Because I want you to be afraid, Jenna. I want you to be very afraid of me."

"I hate you," she spat.

"And do you think Ricky is going to care what happens to you when I tell him you were sleeping with your friend? Who is he, Jenna? DEA? FBI? The pool boy?"

"He's none of your concern," Haley warned in a voice that was low and smooth. "Harm a hair on his head and you'll never see your blood money again."

Luis's laugh was low, throaty and contemptuous. "I will let my brother decide what to do with him. Now may I suggest you retire to the stateroom and shower your lover's scent from your body. Change into something more, shall we say, suitable. You can explain this to Ricky when he arrives."

Haley stood with as much indignation as she could muster. She remained still unable to recall the direction to Ricky's master suite. Her hesitation was mistaken for unwillingness by her host. It seemed to infuriate Luis. She smiled and waited for the blow he wanted to send her way.

"Carlos," he snapped. "Take Jenna to her room and come back to me."

Carlos grabbed Haley's elbow roughly and pushed Haley toward the back of the salon to a set of stairs. They spiraled down to the lower deck.

Jerking free of Carlos, Haley carefully navigated down the stairwell and once below remembered the layout of the cabins. They made their way down the long corridor toward Jenna's and Ricky's stateroom. Carlos side stepped her and opened the door.

Haley slid by him and slammed the door shut. With shaking fingers, she twisted the lock and heard the dead bolt snap into place. She held her breath listening to Carlos who remained just outside her door. Several moments later, she heard his heavy footsteps moving quickly down the hall.

Haley remained at the door, her hands pressed against it. She was alone and for the moment safe. She had infuriated Luis but he did not strike her even though his look had been murderous. If Jenna had fallen out of favor with Ricky, he wouldn't have hesitated to cut her throat. He didn't. He had sent Carlos and Diego who had a grudge of their own to kidnap and terrorize her. While they might have been told to intimidate her, they hadn't truly hurt her in any way. Like Luis they had stopped short. She smiled. Ricky Rojas was still in charge of the Rojas Drug Ring in South Florida. Until he returned, she would be safe.

Turning around, she looked in the elegantly styled master suite. Most luxurious, the master bedroom boasted a large California king size bed. The walls were a stunning night time scene of a tropical beach that wrapped around room in a hand painted mural. Though the painting was motionless, its flow seemed almost real by the gentle sway of the waters below the yacht.

The bedroom had a huge closet, a sitting area with small library and oversized plasma TV. Large windows gave the master suite and the sitting area generous amounts of sunlight. No expense had been overlooked. Haley noted the windows were sealed and offered no escape. At the moment, she didn't want to escape, everything hinged on Ricky's return.

Glancing at herself in Jenna's vanity next to the oversize

dresser, she frowned. Luis had been right about one thing, she needed to freshen up, put on make-up and get herself into one of Jenna's beautiful outfits which hung in the closet.

Midway through her shower, she felt the slightly jarring movement of the yacht as the cruiser left the marina. She quickly shampooed her hair, rinsed herself and stepped out of the shower and into the arms of Ricky Rojas.

Jack slammed his fist into the steering wheel as yet another red light slowed his push to reach the marina. He had used every curse word he knew on the traffic, Ricky Rojas and himself. He blamed himself for not waking. He should have gone for breakfast. She should be safe within his arms.

Traffic cleared in the intersection long enough for him for him to hit the accelerator and steer a course through the interchange. Three more blocks and he turned into the Miami's premier marina. Flooring the beat-up truck, he raced toward the yachts. Haley would be there.

Slamming on the brakes, he bolted from the truck just in time to see a long sleek cruiser leaving the harbor, heading for open sea. Close enough to her stern, he read, El Angel, Bogotá, Columbia.

For the first time in his life, Jack felt his knees weaken. For the first time in his life he knew fear.

With his fists clinched in anger, he heard himself scream, "HALEY!"

"NO!" Haley cried jerking out of Ricky's arms.

Ricky stood silent just staring at her. "What do you mean NO? You stole from me. What did you want the money for? I would have given it to you, Jenna. I make that much money a week! You think I care about the money?"

Haley stood clutching the towel around her. "We need to talk," was all she could manage.

Ricky was as she remembered him; powerful, handsome with black short cropped hair, his profile strong and his head held high with pride. Dressed in a blue silk shirt and dark pants, he looked the same, only his dark fathomless eyes were dark with pain, anger and turmoil.

"Tell me why I shouldn't kill you right now?" He screamed his voice rich in anger. His black eyes were cold and proud and glowed with a savage inner fire above the rim of anger and love.

Haley's voice rose in anger, she had only one weapon to hurl at Ricky Rojas. Finding her voice she said in a whisper, "You love me. As I love you."

Ricky grew strangely quiet. Haley looked up at him just in time to watch his eyes and his resolve soften. "Yes, I love you, Jenna, I will always love you."

Haley tried to move away from him, with only a towel wrapped around her, she was wholly at his mercy.

Suddenly Ricky backed away from her. His dark eyes flashed in gentle warning.

"Come into the bedroom," he said spinning on his heel.

Haley allowed the towel to drop from her moist body and grabbed the smaller of the heavy white bath robes. She followed him into the master suite, gathering the robe over her breasts and silken legs.

Standing fiercely, she dropped her eyes before his steady gaze.

"You almost had me fooled," he said softly. With a clear voice that bridged no quarter he said, "Haley, where is my wife?"

"What?" Haley cried, "You and Jenna are married?"

"A month ago in the Aruba," Ricky said taking a seat across from the bed. "She was going to surprise you in person.

Where is Jenna? Where is my money? And who is that man you are sleeping with?"

Haley had no course but the truth. She had much to explain as she looked at Ricky's too cool demeanor. Before she could begin, Ricky interrupted her, his voice twisting with anguish.

"Why did she leave me?" he begged. "I want to know why she left me."

"She's pregnant," Haley said. "Jenna didn't want the money, she only wanted the child raised away from..."

His dark eyebrows shot up in genuine surprise. "Jenna is pregnant with my son? Why didn't she tell me? Where is she?"

"In a hospital in Key West. She was shot by one of your thugs last night."

The joy on Ricky's face turned to alarm. "DIOS! Is she all right? The baby?"

Haley shook her head. She wanted me to come to you and return the money. She said she would have never told the FBI anything about you. She just wanted to get away."

Ricky looked down at the carpet. When he looked up misty tears were in his eyes. "Is she all right?"

"Yes, it was minor and she's is getting the best of care. Jack said..."

"Who is this Jack?" Ricky interrupted, "Your boyfriend?"

Haley shook her head. "No, he's..."

Ricky studied her face. "This Jack, he is your lover."

"Yes," Haley answered. That would suffice. "Yes, he is my lover."

Ricky relaxed and took a soft breath, his expression growing severe. "How serious is Jenna's wound?"

"Jack said it looked like the bullet went through her shoulder. Ricky, Jenna wanted me to return the money. Let her raise the baby in peace away from the drugs and the crime."

Ricky put his hands together and took a long breath. "This is serious. By stealing the money and going to the FBI she has created a problem for my family."

"I know where the money is if you want it returned."

"The money is truly of little consequence to me; however, her actions have brought my leadership into question. My father and uncles have sent my younger brother here to see that I do what is right."

Haley felt chills race over her skin like fast moving insects. Ricky may have a problem killing his wife but he had just made it clear to her, he would have no qualms in killing her sister.

He took a long breath. "No one seems aware that you have traded places with Jenna. Stay in the cabin. We're on our way to Grand Bahama Island. Jenna hid in a safety deposit box at Hamilton Bank, didn't she?"

Haley nodded. In the end she had no bargaining chips. Still, Ricky and Luis would need her face to get to the safety deposit box. She would be expendable after they retrieved the bonds.

"Let me think, Haley. While I'm not inclined to shoot you or Jenna, Luis will have no hesitation about shooting either of you but not until we have the bond returned. This is a matter of honor, Haley. Returning the money will appease my family some but not completely. You are in danger. I am in danger."

With that he rose and walked across the room and gave her a brotherly hug. "For now, stay in the cabin, don't leave. I'll have dinner sent to you. Tomorrow we'll get the money returned; I will do what I can to placate my family. Having

Jenna pregnant will help. My father has long wanted a grandson. Now this person, your lover Jack, who is he? I have to know."

"Jack Morgan," Haley said slipping away from him. "He's in the witness protection program and has a contract on his head."

Ricky nodded. "I'll do what is necessary to keep you and your sister safe Haley but as Jenna likes to say, we are up to our ass in alligators, Haley. I'll do what I can."

Jack Morgan stood on the dock for over 30 minutes quickly assessing his options. There was no doubt he would go after her. He had no choice. Sure, he would get a plane out of Miami International, he might even get lucky enough to rescue Haley but they would be stranded on an island not under U.S. jurisdiction. He needed mobility. He needed a boat, a fast one.

He called Frank on his cell phone.

CHAPTER ELEVEN

U nder a pale moon and smooth waters, the yacht stayed a steady course to the Bahamas. On board, Haley could do little but sit and watch the mainland fade into the distance. She was leaving everything behind, her life, her sister and Jack.

Her skin still tingled from the feel of his touch. She hungered for the taste his lips upon her mouth and her breasts. The ecstasy of each sweet soft kiss had left her body aching for his touch. In the quiet of the state room, tears burned for such sweetness lost. His face haunted her, smiling, angry, thoughtful, playful as the day turned to night. She relived each moment with him a hundred times and avowed she would die just to touch his handsome face again. The pirate's coin he had brought her stayed tight within her palm, her only hope of salvation, her only memento of love.

Around nine, Ricky had sent Haley a dinner and a small bottle of wine. She ate without tasting the beautifully prepared food; her thoughts clung to Jack and each moment they shared.

She waited for Ricky to return to the master suite but fell asleep around midnight. Ricky entered the bedroom after one and made a feeble attempt to be quiet. He lay down beside her but did not attempt to touch her. When she woke the next morning, he was gone. She woke the next morning to a knock on her door.

"Miss Jenna," a young male voice called out. "Breakfast is served in the sundeck; Senor Rojas asked if you would join him there."

"Yes," Haley called back tossing the covers off of her. Looking out the windows, she could see the yacht was moored in a marina. They had arrived on Grand Bahama Island.

Haley picked out a lovely white silk blouse that shimmered softly with each contour of her shoulders and breasts. She found matching silk pants and was pleased to see that she and Jenna still wore the same size. Jenna kept a full compliment of make-up in the bathroom; Haley picked out her favorites and applied the make-up a bit heavier than usual. Looking stylish and rich, it was easier to assume her sister's pretentious air of sophistication. She slipped the necklace with its pirate's doubloon over her head and hid it next to her skin. Closing her eyes, she clung to the sweet memory of Jack slipping it around her neck. She drew courage from the coin and from Jack praying the coin would bring her luck.

Taking a deep breath, she knew she must play her part well this day. If she did, there was a slim chance she just might come out of this alive. At least, Jenna and Jack were both safe.

Hardly the sacrificial lamb, she opened the door knowing she would have to rely on every analytical skill she possessed over the next several hours. She would stay prepared to whatever was to follow.

She had no escort from the main deck to the upper deck.

On the main deck, she paused and glanced toward the doorway. The gangway could lead her to the U.S. Embassy. It would be easy enough to leave the yacht but the dance had started. She didn't know how this day would end but she had no choice but to play her part and play it well.

She forced herself to move toward the spiral stairwell that led to the sun deck. Besides, she thought with a wry smile, she was confident, Diego or Carlos were ready to block her way if she attempted to leave the ship.

Both Ricky and Luis rose at the sight of her. Polite for murderers, she thought crossing the deck to them.

"Good Morning, my dear," Ricky said with an open smile. If she thought him handsome before, he looked even more striking this morning. When she reached the table, he leaned forward and pressed a light kiss on her cheeks. "You look ravishing, my dear."

Haley smiled and nodded as Jenna would have and allowed Ricky to adjust her chair closer to the table. A young steward dressed in white immediately came to pour her a cup of coffee. Having completed his task, he moved quickly away to his post by a serving table laden with coffee, tea, several juices and three bottles of champagne.

"I have been explaining to my brother," Ricky said taking his seat next to her, "that if he ever harms you, speaks to you in the manner in which he did yesterday, I will kill him."

Though he said it with a smile, the cold look in Ricky's eyes as he glanced over to his brother told her his words, though said in idle conversation, carried a lethal warning. The penalty for harming the wife of Ricky Rojas was death.

Luis crossed his legs and snapped his fingers for the steward to bring him more champagne. Though Luis tried to scoff off Ricky's threat, his eyes narrowed as though he knew the blood bond between them would carry no forgiveness.

"You made yourself a fool for this girl, Ricky." Luis said in a mocking tone as he waited for his glass to be filled. The server filled the glass and Luis downed the champagne as if it were sparkling water. He held his glass out for more before the attendant retreated into to the corner. "You are as soft as an old woman."

Ricky's eyes turned indifferent and he curled into a soft smile. "My brother, when you meet the woman you love, you will love her as our father loves our mother and as I love Jenna. For now I am in charge and you will toast the birth of my son."

Haley looked at Ricky and he lifted his glass to her. Luis threw down his napkin but with Ricky's black eyes upon him, he reluctantly raised his glass."

"As I told you last night, Luis," Ricky said, his tone raw, his will to be followed. "Jenna was under my orders to take the money to the Bahamas. It was not her fault that she was kidnapped by the FBI."

"Kidnapped?" Luis spat. "You think she was kidnapped?"

"I know she was. Now, no more unpleasantness. When Jenna finishes her breakfast, we will go to the bank and retrieve our funds. And you, Luis, will learn a bit more about smuggling money out of the U.S."

Luis bolted from his chair. "I don't believe her or you."

Ricky took a slow sip of his coffee. "When you are in charge of the U.S. operation you can run this as you like. In the meantime, I shall do what I think is best for the family."

Luis downed his glass of champagne. Angry but with no recourse, he stood and walked toward the stairwell, grabbing the bottle of champagne from the steward as he passed.

"Ricky," Haley began softly but Ricky reached across the table and grasped her hand. His eyes silenced her.

"Not now my dear," he said in a hushed whisper. "We must keep our secrets to ourselves. Eat your breakfast; we'll be going to the bank shortly. The sooner Luis is out of the country the better. Can I presume, my dear, you have the key to the safety deposit box?"

"Yes," Haley said her hand automatically reaching up to touch the chain.

"Good," Ricky said, "we will stay here for several days then return to Miami."

Haley said nothing.

"And, this morning I have good news of your sister. She is well and has not lost my son."

Relieved to hear good news of her sister, Haley looked at him. "How were you able to find out?'

"An informant and a very expensive one I might add. Once our situation is resolved here, I'll make arrangements for her to join us."

"Is that how you found me, through an informant?"

"Yes, I knew where you were, almost always. Your Jack is very clever."

Haley gasped. "But the agents, the men in the safe house, the ones that were killed..."

Ricky sipped his coffee and glanced across the marina. "That is regrettable of course but sometimes necessary. Causalities of war."

"I don't approve of your 'business' Haley snapped. "Neither does my sister. Not to change the subject but exactly what did you tell Luis about Jack Morgan?"

"The truth of course," Ricky said with a dazzling smile toward the steward. "That he is a paid security expert who will be rewarded for helping you escape from the FBI. How else could I allow him to live?"

Haley sat silent. Jack would be safe in the lie.

"How were you able to follow my every move and track me so carefully? No one knew where I was at but..."

She stopped as a cold shiver running down the length of her body. Only one man alive knew where she was. Only one man was responsible for the murders of the FBI and Marshals. Only one man who knew she was in the Everglades and somehow guessed her whereabouts in the Keys. Frank Porter. Thank God, Jack was far away from him. Thank God, he was safe.

It had taken the *Wave Dancer* less than three hours to cross the distance from south Florida to Nassau on Grand Bahama Island. With the *Wave Dancer* running at full speed and Frank Porter at the helm they had crossed under fair winds and calm waters over the warm waters of the Gulf Stream. This wasn't Frank's first trip and he knew the way well.

Jack had met Frank back at the Marina in Key Biscayne and after gassing up, taking on a few supplies, they headed directly toward the Bahamas.

He would have preferred to go after Haley alone but Frank made a cool argument. He wanted Ricky Rojas as bad as Jack wanted Haley. Jack didn't care that Frank was going to operate outside of government guidelines; he wanted Ricky Rojas dead and Haley back in his arms. Nothing else, not a damm thing mattered.

Jack watched Frank on the trip; his attention remained on driving of the powerful cigarette across the still waters. Except for asking for a beer, Frank kept the boat at full speed.

Leaning back in the seat, Jack had nothing to do but think. His insides were twisting over Haley. Looking always forward to the distant horizon, he said softly across the miles, "Stay alive Haley, stay alive."

Jack looked at Frank. He had told Frank the money was in a bank in the Bahamas and that she had the key to the safety deposit box. Frank said that by the time this went through proper channels, Ricky, Luis and Haley would be off the island and anywhere.

Jack remembered back to the first time he met Frank. He'd liked him right away. He trusted him; hell, Frank had taken a bullet for him and saved his life. He owed him much and now he was willing to risk his life and his career to help him bring back the woman he loved. If they came back with international drug lords Ricky Rojas and his brother Luis so much the better.

Jack looked at Frank. Frank nodded and waved his beer in salutation, they were approaching the beautiful Grand Bahama Island. He was close to Haley.

Frank seemed to have no qualms moving outside the law for which Jack was grateful.

With Grand Bahama Island rising like an emerald jewel from a turquoise sea, Jack looked ahead.

In a hushed whisper he said, "Haley, stay alive, my love. I will find you. Just stay alive."

A *Hummer* was waiting for them when Luis, Ricky and Haley left the yacht. Climbing in, Haley guessed the bulky vehicle was probably amour plated. She sat next to Ricky and stared out the window. Carlos was at the wheel. Diego sat beside him in the front passenger seat. Their guns were openly displayed.

Ricky was deadly calm, his eyes trading glances between Haley and Luis. An expensive leather attaché case was at this side. Luis opened another bottle of champagne and poured himself a glass without offering it to Ricky or Haley. His smug look sent Haley's temper soaring but she sat silently. Ricky was her protector. Sticks and stones, Haley thought giving Luis a polite smile.

The marina sat on the end of a busy Bahamian marketplace.

The shops were as exclusive as those on Rodeo Avenue and sat side by side with flamboyant tourist shops with open air straw stands offering beautiful multicolored garments and wooden animals.

The air was alive with the festive beat of steel drums and the sweet exotic smell of Caribbean cuisine. People both dark skinned and white mingled in a beautiful array of bright colors, their strides in perfect step to the gay music that was all around them.

Weaving their way through crowed streets, the Hummer stopped almost directly in front of the Hamilton Bank. Carlos stepped out of the car and opened the back door for Luis, Ricky and Haley to exit.

"Señor Rojas, Madam," a smiling bank manager said approaching them. Impeccably dressed in a light gray suit, he had a friendly smile. He gave Haley a polite slight nod in greeting then turned to Luis and Ricky. "I trust your trip was smooth sailing?"

"Yes, Ethan, very nice," Ricky said accepting the Manager's welcoming handshake.

"Well, I know you are very busy today, "the manager said folding his hands and dipping slightly toward them. He held out his arm. "Come this way. Your husband explained that you lost your identification Señora Rojas. If you would please, sign our registry, so that I may compare the signatures. Just a formality, I assure you."

"Yes," Haley said accepting the pen.

"Please," Ethan said motioning to a large oak desk.

Haley tried to steady her hand. Years earlier, switching places meant signing each other's name. Remembering Jenna's teenage script, Haley nervously wrote Jenna's name and stopped. To have been allowed such liberties as securing a safety deposit box without questions, Jenna would have used her new married name. She hastily added Rojas. For a breathless moment, the bank manager compared both signatures then looked to her and Ricky and smiled.

Haley swallowed hard knowing she had used her last bit of luck.

"Your husband may accompany you if you like."

"That is not necessary," Ricky said looking directly at Luis. He handed Haley the attaché case as the bank manager called out to his assistant. "Refreshments, please."

A beautiful Bahamian secretary rose from her desk and scurried off to bring Luis and Ricky some coffee.

Ethan looked at Haley. "Very well, this way please, madam, if you would follow me."

She was taken through a vaulted door past a security guard to a small room filled with stacks of metal boxes. Ethan pulled out one of the long drawers and carried the box to a private viewing table. A small overhead security camera followed their every movement.

"When you are finished, madam; just signal for the guard." Ethan said with a smile. He bowed slightly and then left her alone.

The moment he cleared the door, Haley opened the large box to immediately find a small stash of bonds. How many lives had been ruined, she thought reaching in for the bonds. Opening the attaché case, she placed the bonds in four small stacks. Leaving the box empty, she signaled to the guard who buzzed her out of the room.

Ricky and Luis were standing, talking to Ethan when she returned. Haley passed the attaché case to Ricky.

"I trust everything was satisfactory, Señora Rojas," Ethan said softly with a smile.

Haley nodded.

"Yes, I am assured it is, thank you." Ricky answered for her, pressing a large roll of dollars into the manager's hands. "Ethan, next time we are in the Bahamas, please join me for dinner on the yacht."

The manager's face brightened but he remained reserved. "It would be my great pleasure, Señor Rojas."

With a nod, Ricky reached for Haley's elbow and they turned heading toward the door.

Walking out of the bank, Haley looked about. This would be the perfect time for escape but escaping would endanger Ricky's plans. She tried to keep a steady course knowing her life rested in Ricky's hands.

Passing the lobby, she noticed two couples waiting, one old, one young and a man with a newspaper seated on the elegant white sofas.

As they passed the man seated on a sofa who was reading a newspaper, he dropped the paper beside him. Rising, he stepped in front of Ricky and Haley blocking their path.

"Take the money," Jack Morgan said evenly to Ricky Rojas. "Leave the girl."

CHAPTER TWELVE

His dark eyes were steady, cold and his lips sealed tight with fury. He stood poised and made no attempt to veil his warning. "You don't want any trouble, Rojas. You got what you came for. Leave her with me."

"Jack," Haley said in a voice that was soft and clear. Her breath quickened as she felt a cold fist closing over her heart. Her arm held firmly within Ricky's gasp, she dared not move as Ricky tightened his fingers into her flesh.

As man used to living on death's edge, Ricky's remained still, his eyes slightly narrowed, his mouth thinned with displeasure. If he had been caught off guard, he didn't show it. He mouth twisted wryly. "Jack Morgan, we are meeting at the most inopportune moment."

"This is her lover." Luis hissed. "He is threatening you. Shoot him."

Ricky glanced at Luis and gave him an indulgent smile. "We are not in Columbia, my brother, shooting him in the middle of this bank would draw unnecessary attention to ourselves and our good friends at this financial institution."

Jack inched closer to Ricky.

"Take the money," he warned, a circle of ice ringing his mouth. "Leave this woman to me."

Ricky smiled, his expression was a mask of stone. "You are a very brave man, my friend and a very foolish one to challenge me like this. You love her as I do my Jenna."

Ricky's subtle message resonated through Jack like a knife twisting its way from his heart down his spine. Assessing the man before him, Jack realized Ricky knew the woman in his grasp was Haley, not Jenna.

"If you don't want to shoot him in the bank," Luis spat his body shaking with rashness. "Then take him out to the streets. What are you waiting for?"

Ricky and Jack looked at one another. Haley stood transfixed in horror knowing her life and the life of the man she loved hung in the balance.

An astonishing sadness passed over Ricky like a foreboding shadow. "So, this woman means so much to you that you would risk your life to take her from me?"

"Or die trying," came Jack's quick reply.

Luis's brows furrowed deeply. The veins on his neck stood out in livid ridges, as his face grew red with blood lust. "You let this man speak to like this you about your wife!"

Carlos and Diego entered the bank in unison. Both pulled semiautomatics from inside their coats and brandished their weapons at the four of them. Women screamed and the men standing nearest them recoiled in horror, eyes darting for a place to hide.

In one fluid movement, Jack turned and pulled a glock out from the waistband of his pants. Tellers and secretaries screamed in terror and hid behind desks.

Standing in front of Haley and Ricky, Jack held his gun steady. Carlos and Diego remained on the three of them as Luis slowly stepped away from the group.

"You intend to assassinate me, my brother?" Ricky said with a glance toward Luis.

Haley watched in numbed horror as Luis joined the

two Columbians by the entrance. His black eyes sparkled in pleasure and his eyes narrowed in disdain.

"I should be in charge, Ricky," Luis said, his lips curling in disgust, "not you. This woman has made you weak, Enrique. With you dead, I will be put in charge of South Florida and the US."

Ricky remained expressionless. "You would spill your brother's blood? And in front of so many witnesses who will report back to our father, Luis?"

"Yes, and I will run the U.S. operation for our family, Ricky."

"This is your plan, Luis?" Ricky said articulating each word with deadly accuracy.

Luis Rojas stared at his brother. Hatred, envy and malice shone bright in his dark eyes.

Luis, Carlos and Diego stood facing Ricky, Jack and Haley. Their attention switched from the mussel of Jack's gun to Ricky. Though they had thrown their allegiance to Luis, they stood hesitant and mindful that they were about to shoot the beloved son of Columbian's deadliest drug lord.

"Ethan," Ricky asked to the bank manager. "Is there a back way out?"

"Yes, Señor. There is a door; straight to the back of the building."

"Sounds like a plan," Jack said moving in slow motion in front of Ricky and Haley. With his single mission to get Haley out of the bank alive, Jack moved in front of Ricky and Haley. "Get her out of here. NOW!"

The moment Ricky moved, Diego fired at him but the bullet shattered the base of a large fern. Jack fired twice at the Columbians, giving Ricky and Haley precious moments of cover fire. Ricky pushed Haley toward the back of the bank; Jack followed dodging the gunfire in his direction.

Pandemonium echoed in screams and gunfire as Diego, Carlos and Luis ran through the bank after them.

"Now what?" Ricky asked once they were safely out of the bank. He looked up and down the alley as if gauging their next course of escape.

A sedan squealed as it turned into the alley. Racing toward them, it came to a screeching stop beside them. At the wheel, Frank Porter yelled. "GET IN!"

Ricky yanked open the front door as Jack jerked opened the back door. Helping Haley in, Jack slammed the door shut. Frank hit the gas pedal, sending a surge of power through the sedan. Ricky grabbed the passenger door and closed it as the door's rim hit several trash cans.

They were halfway down a narrow block when Diego and Carlos emerged from the back of the bank and began firing at them.

Careening down the narrow streets, Frank pulled onto the main thoroughfare almost hitting a taxi as he made a hairpin turn.

"It's not safe for you to be here, Ricky," Frank said driving wilding through the crowded streets. "If you want to live we need to get you back to the US Mainland. You can deal with this there."

Ricky nodded. "My yacht is…"

"Too slow," Frank said keeping a steady hand on the wheel. "We have a boat waiting and gassed at the marina. We can be back in Miami in three hours. Where are the bonds?"

Ricky held up the attaché case and braced himself as Frank turned into the south end of the marina.

"Good," Frank said with a sudden smile. "We're gassed up and ready to leave."

With her heart pounding, Haley looked at Jack. Relieved to be away from Carlos and Diego, they were not out of danger. Jack squeezed her hand but his touch offered little assurance.

Jack hid his smile as he listened to Frank's explanation. How easily Ricky was playing into his hands. Ricky Rojas one of the deadliest drug lords in South Florida would be in the custody of the U.S. Marshals office before sunset.

So close to Frank and Ricky, Haley dared not breathe her certainty that Frank Porter was working with the Rojas Drug Cartel.

Jack watched the flickering warning lights in Haley's eyes as she glanced at Frank Porter. Mindful they were in a foreign country and involved in a shoot out left him little doubt that right or wrong, they needed to leave the island. At the moment, he had no choice but to trust Frank and his instincts that he could keep Haley safe.

As they reached the marina, Frank pulled into the parking lot and left the keys in the ignition. They were leaving, and they weren't coming back.

"This way," Frank said motioning them to the end of the dock where the *Wave Dancer* lay in readiness for a quick departure.

As not to draw further attention to themselves, Frank with Ricky walked leisurely to the end of the dock.

"Jack," Haley cried in a hoarse whisper.

"I know," Jack said pulling her along. "But we have no other choice, Haley. Between the Bahamian Government and Luis and company, we have to get the hell off this island."

Just before they reached the Wave Dancer, he turned and said, "I love you."

With her eyes glistening in tears, her heart swelling with love and fear, she looked to Jack, suddenly filled with hope. "I love you Jack."

Jack squeezed her hand, his eyes glowing warm, gloried in one brief private moment of elation.

Frank jumped into the center of the boat. Ricky gracefully jumped on board and immediately began untying the boat from the mooring. Jack climbed in and lifted Haley from the dock placing her gently upon a seat behind the helm. Ricky climbed back to the cockpit as Jack released the bow lines.

Frank fired the ignition and the powerful motor drew attention throughout the marina. Ricky opened the locker which housed the life jackets and dropped the attaché case on top of them.

Frank glanced at Ricky then to Jack before he began moving the Wave Dancer out away from the dock. Keeping a slow but steady speed, he didn't release the powerful cigarette until they reached the break water.

Jack pulled Haley beside him and held her there while the four made a fast and speedy race west to the U.S. coastline.

The roar of the engines allowed little room for conversation. An hour and a half into the trip, Ricky found beers in the cooler and he graciously passed them around. Frank standing at the helm accepted the beer but kept his attention on the break neck speed and windy waters before the formidable cruiser.

Nearing the coast of Florida, Frank slowed the cruiser to a slow idle then stopped. The shining cities of Miami and Ft. Lauderdale glistened under the South Florida sun. Frank slowly turned to Ricky.

"Why are we stopping?" Ricky asked, his voice was curious but held no alarm.

"Because," Frank said slowly. "This is where everyone gets off."

The boat rocked gently on top of the waves as they moved to the shoreline.

"What the hell are you doing? I know you don't expect us to swim to shore," Jack said looking across the water.

Frank half smiled and pulled a gun from the boat's console. His eyes were hooded and there was a cold edge in his voice. "You won't have to."

Ricky who had been seated stood and positioned himself closer to Haley.

"Frank, there is no need to harm Haley or Jack, if it's the money you want, then..."

"You're right," Frank interrupted him in a mocking tone. "It's the money I want. You see after thirty-three years of dedicate service, I'm supposed to retire and live off a government pension. I have eight million dollars at my disposal; I have only one small problem, the three of you."

"Frank," Jack spat, "What the hell are you doing? You took a bullet for me."

Frank sneered. "I didn't take a bullet for you, Jack. I pushed you away so I could get a clear shot at Vinnie the Rat. He was shooting at me, you moron, not you. I worked for the Vegas Mob long before you came into the picture. Thanks for making me out the hero, pal."

Frank looked at Ricky. "Amigo, it's been a great ride. Jack, you've been a friend. Sorry it has to end this way. Haley, what can I say? Wrong place, wrong time. Jenna should be standing in your shoes and I wanted her there."

Ricky snorted in anger and clinched his fist but it was Haley who cried in anger, "What are you saying?"

"This was my plan all along to get the money and Jenna.

Plans changed. You're twins, damn good looking ones; we could hook up and…"

"Go to hell," Haley snapped.

"What makes you think I'm going to stand here and let you shoot us?" Jack asked in a contemptuous tone. "There are two of us, Frank. Shoot Ricky, I'll kill you. Shoot me, Ricky will kill you. Either way, you're a dead man if you try to go through with this."

Ricky glanced at Jack and nodded. "He's right, Frank. Put the gun down, you aren't going to get away with this."

"Really?" Frank asked. His voice was playful but his eyes were cold as ice. "Actually, I think I've done a pretty good job of covering my tracks so far. No one even knows I was on Grand Bahama Island. No one knows I have the eight million. The only two seen with you were Jack Morgan and Haley Rollins."

"So now what? You expect us to swim to shore?" Jack asked moving forward slightly. He was closer to Frank. Haley sensed he was only buying time.

"You're not going to swim anywhere, Jack," Frank said with a laugh. His intent was clear. They were all going to die.

"Now everyone, get your hands in the air. Who's first?"

Jack took a step forward, raised his arms higher causing his shirt to rise. He glanced at Ricky then back behind himself, his eyes motioning toward the revolver in his waistband.

"It doesn't have to be this way, Frank," Jack warned moving closer still. "You can let us go. Hell, look at least let Haley go."

"Always so friggin' noble, Jack," Frank said pointing the gun at Jack's head. "You want to be first?"

As Frank pulled back the trigger, Ricky slipped the gun from Jack's waist, and leveled it at Frank. He fired the gun without hesitation.

Frank screamed and looked down at the blood running from his chest.

"You shot me," he said as the gun fell from his hand onto the deck. He stepped backwards and then fell into the water. Blood trickled out of his mouth as he reached for the side of the boat but the water was turning red around him. With his eyes open, he sank into the Gulf Steam.

Haley screamed and leaned over the boat in a desperate attempt to grab Frank but Ricky pulled her away from rail. His eyes were cold as they watched Frank sink into the darkness. "There is nothing you can do for him Haley. Dead men tell no tales."

Jack picked up Frank's gun and looked at Ricky Rojas.

"Jack, no," Haley cried stepping in front of Ricky. "He saved my life, Jack, he kept me alive."

"Which puts me in a difficult place," Jack said. "Haley's right. You've put me in the middle of a moral dilemma. You have eight million dollars of drug money in your possession, and are a known drug trafficker."

Ricky smiled and gently moved Haley away from him. "If you want to shoot me, go ahead."

Jack grinned and dropped the gun to his side. "I can't. It would make for awkward family gatherings."

Ricky smiled and reached out his hand. Jack grasped it firmly and shook Ricky's hand. "You will come to visit me when my son is born?"

Jack nodded. With a glance toward shore, Jack said, "We better get out of here before the coast guard shows up."

"What about Frank?" Haley protested looking down at the water.

Jack looked at Haley. "Dead men tell no tales."

Ricky went to the console and fired the boat's powerful

engine. Running slow, he brought the boat back into Key Biscayne Marina.

"I'll let you off here," Ricky said pulling up to an empty slip. "Jack, I'd like to offer you a reward."

Jack shook his head. "No thanks, I work for my money."

Haley looked at Ricky. "Are you going to be okay?"

"Yes," Ricky said giving her a quick hug. "I'm going to be okay. I have the money and I will deal with my Father. He has long wanted a grandson and I'm tired of this business. It has almost cost me a wife."

Jack got out of the boat and offered his hand to Haley. The minute she was off, Ricky waved and slowly took craft out of the marina. Haley guessed he was going to the Rojas Compound before disposing of the boat for good.

Watching Ricky leave, Jack turned to her and in a low silvery voice said, "Honey, we can't go back now, if we do, we'd have to tell the truth and right now, I don't know what the truth is. Maybe I should have turned Ricky in but for once, I have no regrets."

"Where are you going to go?" Haley said softly.

"Well, we're going to go to the first motel I can find and continue what we started last night. After that, we're going to buy more clothes, get passports and head to Greece. I think I already mentioned I have a standing job offer there. Have you ever been to Greece, Haley?"

Haley shook her head. He had said "we." Tears glistened on her lovely heart shaped face. Before she could say a word Jack swept her weightlessly into his arms. With his mouth a breath away from hers, he said, "You're going to love it there."

"I love you, Jack Morgan," she said to the magnificent man in her arms.

"And I," Jack said as he brought his lips down over hers, "love you too."

EPILOGUE

Haley looked out of her villa and smiled. She could see Jack and their three year old son Ryan walking toward the Hotel's private vineyard and couldn't recall a time when she felt happier or more at peace.

Watching her husband and her son, she had yet to tell Jack that another son or daughter was on the way.

She put down the letter that just arrived and smiled. Who would have thought Jenna the ultimate party girl would be a matronly mother of three daughters living happily in the south of Spain with her adoring husband, Ricky.

She frowned remembering the day Ricky had left them on the dock in South Florida. Things were so uncertain that day, but Jack did exactly what he said he was going to do and her son Ryan was the proof of it arriving six months after Jenna's and Ricky's child.

Frank Porter, she thought with a frown. She hadn't thought of him in years. His body was never found.

Ricky had been demoted and in time was joined by his wife Jenna. They were allowed to live. Luis had assumed leadership over the U.S. drug operation but his reign hadn't lasted long. He was now serving several connective life sentences in a federal prison far away from the bright lights he had craved.

Within her a new life stirred restlessly.

Outside the window, she watched Jack lift Ryan up on his back to carry him. She heard Ryan's wild giggles and smiled.

In the end, Haley realized, sometimes heroes like Jack are not all good and sometimes men like Ricky Rojas are not all bad.

Sometimes, they are simply pirates.

The End

ABOUT THE AUTHOR

Since exploding into the world of suspense, Linn Random has achieved top reviews for her novels. Her name is linked to spine tingling suspense, action-packed excitement and characters that sparkle with intensity and emotion. Her novels are fresh with multi-layered plots that will leave you breathless.

Linn Random lives in Central Florida with her husband, son and two cats Kirby and Lara. Linn is a K-9 Search and Rescue Volunteer and works with her beloved SAR dog Hunter.

She has been featured in numerous interviews in print and radio and is a prominent national speaker.

Linn is a member of the Mystery Writers of American, International Thriller Writers, Sisters in Crime and the Romance Writers of America.

If you love heart pounding danger and cover to cover action with beautiful, resourceful heroines and street savvy men who will leave your pulses racing, you will enjoy Linn Random's romantic suspense novels in print, ebook and audio format.

For a FREE Chapter Reads, watch "Movie Trailers",
Complete Reviews, Audio Books and Contest Prizes visit
www.LinnRandom.com

ALSO BY LINN RANDOM
Lights, Camera. Murder!

A Reality TV Show that needs a Real CSI
5 Hearts, 5 Stars, 5 Cups of Coffee, 5 Blue Ribbons, 5
Unicorns

Just seventy miles north of Tampa, on Florida's Gulf Coast, St. Gabrielle offers McMasters Studio the perfect locale for this third in a series of reality 'whodunits' that allows the TV audience to follow along in week to week episodes. Isolated and surrounded by water on three sides, the location supervisor had assured the Studio it was the perfect place *for murder.*

In the Gulf of Mexico...

Too late, Sage realized she should have waited for Jon.

"I don't feel well," she heard herself say.

"Come sit down," he said softly, "I'll get you a glass of water."

Allowing him to guide her back to her seat, she was trying desperately to shake off the queasiness.

The sharks were now circling the boat. More than she could count. Their speed was increasing; the water was boiling with their movement.

With her heart pounding, her breath ragged, she watched as his face contorted grotesquely changing into to someone she didn't know.

She stiffened at his touch, loathing his hand upon her.

Fear was welling inside as she tried desperately to wake her dulled senses.

She glanced at the Mimosa as she struggled to fight off the effects of whatever drug he had hidden in the sweet orange mixture.

He gave her a monstrous glare then his face sharpened in disgust. His eyes took on a haunted expression and she realized what she should have seen long ago.

He was insane.

"I'm going to hate doing this."

"What are you going to do?" Sage asked with a forced smile. The sharks were swimming faster. They smelled blood.

The veins in his neck tightened in a stubborn line and his smile was malicious. His eyes regarded her in bitter triumph.

"Why, Sage," he said slowly, his voice was dipping with spite, "I thought you might have guessed by now. The home audience is going to watch you die."

ALSO BY LINN RANDOM
Your Cheatin' Hearts
A Lucille Ball Comedy with a Twist of Magnum P.I.
The Ecataromance 2005 Reviewers Choice of the Year in
Comedy
5 Stars, 5 Cupids, 5 Unicorns, Recommended Reads

Combine one hair brain undercover assignment with two bungling kidnappers and get the most eligible bachelor in town. It's a recipe for disaster for pretty PI Shelby MacGregor who always gets her man.

EXCERPT:

"Mrs. Colter," Shelby MacGregor said trying not to sound impatient, "on the phone you said this was urgent, a matter of life and death."

"Did I say that?" Maggie Colter stammered almost as if taken by surprise. She seemed a bit confused and quiet as though she were contemplating her reply.

Shelby remained silent. Meeting a private investigator for the first time made a lot of people nervous. In three years of heading her own agency, *Your Cheatin Hearts*, she knew she could learn a lot by nervous chatter as well as gain valuable insight into a client' personality. This was crucial, for if their spouse was found cheating, it was imperative she know how her clients would react.

Maggie Colter was different, she had no spouse. She did,

however, need her help. Her call came just this morning. It was a matter of life or death she had pleaded. Now Maggie Colter sat hesitant and unresponsive.

Moments passed. Shelby sat patiently. Maggie was hiding something. What? More important why?

Suddenly Maggie Colter's eyes widened, her round face lit with delight. "Yes! That's it! My son is in definite danger, Ms. MacGregor."

The image of Jack Colter flashed in Shelby's mind. The ruggedly handsome Jack Colter looked like a man who could take care of himself.

"You son is in danger?" Shelby repeated. She heard the doubt in her own voice and she had the nagging suspicion that Maggie Colter was making her story up as she went along.

*E*njoy more spine tingling action, adventure, romance and suspense in 2006 with these exciting Romances from Linn Random.

Haunted Hearts—Summer 2006

Beautiful Psychic Medium Devin O'Shea must fight both a poltergeist and a handsome nonbeliever if she is to help the trapped spirit of a 1920's flapper girl. This scary-sexy romp is a laugh out loud adult comedy and a haunting romance.

Black Waters—Fall 2006

Black Waters is a sexy physiological thriller set in Louisiana Bayou Country where Investigative Reporter Jet Williams is researching the resurgence of Voodoo in the old south. Brent Broussard is a Police Chief in over his head. Together they find their way through a series of terrifying events, Masquerades Balls and steamy cypress swamps. Both Jet and Brent have their own private agendas for unmasking this terrifying cult. Into the Black Waters of they search without realizing…they've become the next targets.

Cold River Murders—2007

Beautiful Mallory McCall has moved to Northern California to escape the glitz, the glamour and the crime in LA. Her life is confined to writing screenplays and working with her K-9 Search and Rescue Team whose searches are limited to missing hikers, lost hunters and an occasional Alzheimer's patient....until one of her dogs finds a graveyard left by a serial killer along the banks of Cold River.

For FREE Chapter Reads, watch "Movie Trailers, Reviews, Contests And more visit www.LinnRandom.com

www.ingramcontent.com/pod-product-compliance
Lightning Source LLC
Chambersburg PA
CBHW061136200626
46817CB00016B/1666